"What brings you to Whiskey Springs?" I asked a bit nervously. I was not prepared for him to say he was searching for me, but it seemed like the logical thing to ask. And blending in, being logical, was very important.

"Work," he said.

Work. I tamped down the bolt of alarm that shot through my system.

But then he grinned at me and my heart rate skittered.

Whether he was the one looking for me or not, I was in trouble.

I was supposed to lay low. Stay out of sight.

Not get attached.

A SECRET ROYAL
CHRISTMAS

Just Maybe
Just Pretend
Just Because

A SECRET ROYAL CHRISTMAS

THE WORTHINGTONS

KATHRYN KALEIGH

To learn more about Kathryn Kaleigh, visit

www.kathrynkaleigh.com

Kathryn Kaleigh

PROLOGUE

The icy cold wind coming off the Canadian bay whipped at her red cashmere scarf, stinging her eyes, and making her ears ache.

Noelle LaFleur was just a girl on a boat. A girl bundled up in a charcoal gray woolen fur-lined hooded cape, gloves, a scarf around her neck. She looked like any other traveler catching the last ferry out to the mainland before sundown.

It had been so easy to slip away as everyone scurried around getting ready for the New Year's Eve festivities scheduled for tonight.

The New Year's Eve celebration was one of many things LaFleur Island did in a grand fashion. Second only to their week of Christmas festivities.

She stood on the top floor of the ferry. The bottom level was for cars. She'd always found that odd because cars were not allowed on LaFleur Island. Only wagons and carriages pulled by horses.

Nothing motorized. There were two snowmobiles used for emergencies, but they, luckily, were rarely used.

So she imagined the cars simply riding back and forth across the bay.

She stared down into the dark swirling water reflecting the last of the muted evening sunlight, the boat pushing its way through a light layer of ice—a harbinger of the winter that was to come.

In the harshest of winters, the island would be inaccessible except by airplane. That was rare though and there was almost always a ferry at least once a day even in the winter.

Noelle had not planned to look back. She had only planned to go forward. But as the ice cold wind burned her face, she turned.

She turned and looked back at the island where she had grown up. A layer of snow covered everything giving it a serene, glistening appearance. The wind tugged her hair loose, whipping it wildly across her face.

From here, nestled in the bluffs, among the forest of trees— pine, spruce, and fir—she could just catch a glimpse of the stone castle where she had grown up. And a castle it was. Thirteen bedrooms. Nineteen fireplaces. Twenty-three cabins on the island for staff housing.

At some time in the past, the cabins had belonged to subjects of the island's king who lived in the castle.

They still called it Castle LaFleur, a remnant from the days when her ancestors had ruled the island. Her great grandparents had been the king and queen of LaFleur Island.

That meant that technically, Noelle was a Princess. Technically nothing more than a bloodline and a title, but nonetheless, she had grown up as any modern princess would have. She'd been tutored in every subject imaginable. She could ride a horse, dance a waltz, and work complex math problems. Her only real deficit was social interaction with others her age.

The island had no industry. Just wealth handed down through the generations. Wealth that naturally dwindled over time. Noelle's grandfather had been an investor and had reversed the inevitable flow during his lifetime.

But Noelle's parents had not lived frugally. They had, in fact, lived extravagantly. Travel. Parties. Yachts. They enjoyed a rich and flashy lifestyle that did not extend so much to their two children.

But it was so much so that the family was now in danger of losing everything. The castle. Even the island itself.

Investors circled the island like hawks. The island would make a perfect resort. The castle—their home—would be an exclusive and lovely hotel. The cabins nestled in the trees would make cozy guest cabins.

Her father, a bold man who made bold decisions that sometimes did not include the sensibilities of others had devised a way to save the island from being bought by investors.

He would marry his only daughter—Noelle—to the son of a wealthy neighbor. The term neighbor being used loosely, since the neighbor in question lived on an island half a day's boat ride away.

Noelle was not clear on just how this would keep the island in the family, but somehow her father had worked it out. Or so he said.

Her younger brother, Nicholas, was only fifteen-years-old, so fortunately he was not of much use in her father's machinations.

Noelle turned her back on the island. Back facing the wind, letting her hair stream behind her. She attempted to adjust her scarf, but quickly returned her hands back to the warmth of the fur-lined pockets.

She had grown tired, so tired, of pleading with her father to change his mind. She had never even met the neighbor's son. This was the twenty-first century, for God's sake.

So she had packed a valise, withdrawn the maximum funds she had quick access to, and took matters into her own hands.

Her only regret was leaving behind her brother, Nicholas.

1

NOELLE LAFLEUR

Dear Nicholas,

I so look forward to the day when you can join me. It's beautiful here in Whiskey Springs, but I have no one to talk to. And even if I did, I could never be completely honest. Not with pretending to be someone else.

— Noelle, written to her younger brother ten months ago, when she first arrived in Whiskey Springs

*U*sing both hands, I pulled a steel tub of vanilla ice cream out of the deep freezer in the back and closed the door with my shoulder.

With a little yelp, I practically dropped it onto the counter and rubbed my hands together. I was always forgetting my mittens. You'd think I would learn after grabbing enough frozen tubs with my bare hands.

Hands burning, I tucked them, a little late, into my warm red frost-proof mittens and picked up the tub again.

It was time to hire some more help, but it was next to impossible to find someone reliable, making the hiring process an exceptionally unpleasant chore. Even tonight, the college student I'd hired called in, claiming a sore throat. Conveniently and suspiciously on the night of the Christmas Tree Festival going on at the high school gym.

I didn't mind working behind the counter. Customers could be trying, but I didn't have to really talk to anyone. REALLY talk to them. Sure, I talked to customers all day long.

We talked about *them.* I knew about high school graduations. Who was dating who. Engagements. Even marital spats.

But to everyone in town, I was just the girl who ran the ice cream parlor. A lot of customers who didn't come in very often or weren't very astute assumed I was merely a server and a cashier. That was okay, too. Actually, it was even better.

After settling the ice cream bucket in its spot in the chilled display case, I straightened, my elbows on the counter, and studied the customers.

Just three days before Christmas and business was booming at my little shop, Smedley's Ice Cream Parlor, in downtown Whiskey Springs, Colorado, just west of Denver.

Whiskey Springs was a little town nestled up high in the heart of the Rocky Mountains. The town was synonymous with Christmas. Starting the first of November, everything turned festive.

Twinkling, colorful Christmas lights draped across everything that didn't move. Garland around every window and door. Piped Christmas music along the sidewalks. Notices sent to businesses reminding us to set our own music to holidays tracks. To put up and decorate our trees. The more decorations the better.

My shop, with a baker's dozen of little round tables, had only two empty at the moment. Definitely a good day for the business.

Some of the tables were painted red with matching chairs. The other half were painted white. The table and chairs were better suited to older children, but adults sat in them all the time, some more easily than others.

Both of the empty tables were on either side of the door. It was a consistent pattern. One I'd been contemplating different solutions to. Customers tended to sit at the back tables first and fill their way toward the front. Happened every time.

Could be that there was no solution to it. Maybe it was just a thing. Maybe if I actually knew more about retail than I did, I might know the answers.

Since this was the night of the Christmas Tree Festival, I should be getting ready to roll my hot chocolate machine cart to the high school gym along with a tub of vanilla ice cream. But not tonight. Tonight business was too good here to leave unattended. Besides, people would find their way here after the tree festival. Instead of me going to them as the previous owner had done, I would let them come to me.

I watched two grade school age girls sitting with their father. I had to give the father credit. He was looking a bit uncomfortable in the smaller chairs, but he was holding his own.

They sat next to the Christmas tree I'd decorated on Thanksgiving Day. I'd spent the whole day on it. Did it all by myself. It didn't look half bad if I had to say so myself.

It wasn't exactly a traditional tree. It had mostly clusters of red berries and pinecones and little birds I'd ordered over the Internet perched among the limbs. But the colorful twinkling lights pulled it all together nicely.

It was the first tree I had ever decorated by myself from start to finish.

One of the teenage boys came up, ordered a hot chocolate milk shake, and I got to work.

The milkshakes were easy to make. Most anything was easy when a person had the right machinery.

And I had the right machinery.

After the teenager slid his credit card, I handed him his milkshake with two straws and he took it back to his table where his pretty teenage girlfriend waited.

Their gazes never left each other's as they used the straws to sip on either side of the drink. It didn't take more than a few seconds before they decided the hot chocolate was too hot to sip through the straws and, their heads bent together in laughter, they moved to spoons.

I wiped my hands on a towel and looked around the little shop.

Nothing out of the ordinary.

Except that it was.

Someone had slipped inside, without me noticing, and was sitting at the table on the right just inside the door. Somehow, probably while I was making the milkshake, I'd missed hearing the little bell over the door that jingled when anyone came inside or left.

He was a man I hadn't seen before. It didn't definitely mean he was a local, but it decreased his chances.

It meant he was probably a tourist.

Whiskey Springs got lots of tourists. That part was nothing unusual. Tourists came mostly in the summer and this week— the week of Christmas. Whiskey Springs had plenty of activities during this week when most places had already run through theirs by now.

He was one of those men who was a little too big for the little red table and chair.

Dropping my damp towel on the counter, I leaned both palms flat against the smooth glass and watched him without being obvious about it. It was something I was good at. I watched people all the time and they never had a clue.

The man hadn't ordered anything and didn't appear to be interested in doing so.

His attention was on his phone.

He was scowling at it mostly. Texting occasionally.

As I watched him, I decided maybe he wasn't a tourist after all. Most tourists wore blue jeans and flannel shirts. Some even wore cowboy hats. Ironically, locals didn't usually wear hats at all, unless it was a warm wool hat.

This guy wore black slacks and a white shirt beneath his light gray woolen coat.

I realized with a start that I was out of practice.

I should have realized that he was dressed differently than other tourists right off.

Immediately going into processing mode, I began going through my mental list of possibilities.

A businessman. Here on some kind of business. A little unusual, considering it was three days before Christmas.

Not a salesman. He didn't have the salesman look about him. A salesman would be paying attention to the other customers.

Same with a reporter. Reporters were always looking around, too. Always paying attention to those around them.

Whoever he was, he was most definitely too handsome for his own good.

The little bell over the door jingled, drawing my attention away from the man sitting alone. Although he wasn't ordering anything, he didn't appear to be any kind of danger, so I focused on the middle-aged couple who came up and asked for two of my famous hot chocolate milk shakes.

2

GREYSON FLEMING

*M*y brother was on his honeymoon.

Normally that would do nothing to disrupt my day. Except that today it did.

My brother Daniel was supposed to have gotten married last summer, but for some reason, unbeknownst to me, he and his fiancé had decided to wait until the week before Christmas to tie the knot.

And now… now it looked like I was going to be stuck here until tomorrow.

I'd flown the company Phenom airplane up here to pick up one of the regular clients, a retired pilot who, unfortunately, was losing his eyesight, to fly him to his daughter's house in Seattle.

That's what we did—my brother and I. We both worked as pilots for Skye Travels.

Skye Travels was our Grandpa Noah's company. Noah Worthington started Skye Travels with one small jet and now his private airline company was an empire rivaling that of any of the major airlines in the country. When newly licensed pilots applied for jobs, the most coveted job was working for Skye Travels. More so than taking a job flying commercial jets.

Grandpa was a true entrepreneur in every sense of the word. He saw opportunities and fearlessly took advantage of them.

It was strange how things worked out. I could not imagine how a person could be part of the Worthington family and not believe in fate.

Grandpa's good friend, Doc Alexander, who lived in Whiskey Springs had reached out to Grandpa about investing in a private airline terminal here. Grandpa explored it and determined that it was a valid need. People were driving all the way to the Denver airport just to board a private jet.

Before the project was even completed, my oldest brother had found his soulmate. Here. Even though neither of them lived here at the time, they met here, were married here, and were planning to make their lives here.

Grandpa, as was his nature, had bought a new Phenom airplane to be housed here in Whiskey Springs with my brother, Daniel, its pilot.

Grandpa had done this so many times over the years, I didn't even know just how many airplanes he owned that were docked at small airports across the country.

With my brother on his honeymoon, the responsibility for the Whiskey Springs airplane fell to me.

And even though my brother apologized profusely for this all happening right at Christmastime, he didn't budge. His wife wanted to be married at Christmastime, so that's what they did.

Daniel did anything his new wife asked. Fortunately for him, she was not very demanding. Except for the wedding, of course.

In the meantime, I was stuck here.

Houston, born and bred, I'd had to cancel my commitments for a few days.

In all honesty, I didn't really mind that part as much as I minded the possibility of not being with my family at Christmas.

I had a girlfriend—sort of. She was more a girlfriend of convenience than anything else.

Our families knew each other, so we ran in the same circles. Mostly we went to functions, like Christmas parties together, but lately she'd been hinting around at the possibility of a commitment.

Since her parents were friends of my parents, I had to tread carefully there and belatedly I saw the danger in taking advantage of that convenience.

To her I was more than a convenience.

A new message came in. My client asked—sort of asked—more like demanded—to be rescheduled. Said something came up. As a well-paying client, he could do that.

And now we weren't going to be flying out today at all.

So I was stuck here.

I slipped out of the cold wind into the first warm shop I'd come to—a little ice cream shop—to answer some text messages. The first thing I had to do was to let the office know that I was having to reschedule my flight. Then I had to let Tiffany know that I was going to be missing the charity function tonight. As I typed the text to Tiffany, I felt an unexpected sense of relief.

Interesting.

I scowled as the message from my client came in confirming that we weren't leaving until morning. I'd figured as much.

I had to get myself a room for tonight and from the number of people walking up and down the street, that might be something of a challenge.

I tried googling a place to stay, but I didn't come up with anything. I would have to ask someone. I might be a guy, but I was not opposed to asking for directions… or a place to stay the night.

As a pilot, I'd spent as many days away from home as I had at home over the past couple of years. It most definitely changed a man's perspective on things.

It taught a man just much he could get by without.

I lived in a modest apartment, even though my other siblings lived in high-rise condos, one of the buildings was even owned by my family.

Needing to secure a place to stay before it got too late, I looked up from my phone.

I'd honestly thought this was a coffee shop—should have been paying better attention—but it was actually an ice cream shop.

Like everything else in Whiskey Springs, it looked like Christmas sprung out of a box and spilled all over everything. Inside and outside. Outside, the door and windows were lined with garland and clear blinking lights. Inside, a large tastefully decorated blue spruce tree stood in one of the two windows. From the pungent scent of the spruce, I could tell it was live. It, too, sparkled with clear twinkling lights. Not a lot of decorations on it. Some red berry bunches, white cardinals with long fluffy tails, and some red cardinals. A big white owl ornament with lots of soft looking feathers sat on the top—the tree topper—overseeing its domain.

I'd never seen a tree decorated quite like this, but it was clean and tasteful looking.

I liked it.

Since I'd been using the little table for my work, I should buy something. A sign on the counter advertised hot chocolate ice cream. Couldn't imagine what that was, but I was always willing to try something new.

While I was at the counter, I'd ask the clerk if she knew of anyplace in town where I could get a room for the night.

All I needed was just one night. Then, hopefully, if my client cooperated, I'd be out of here in the morning. Back to Houston to spend Christmas with my family.

The girl behind the counter turned to face me as I walked her way.

Her eyes widened and she stood perfectly still, but otherwise, she showed no reaction.

I, on the other hand, had a clear and remarkable—as my brother the physician would phrase it—reaction.

In fact, I had never had such a reaction to anyone.

The girl looked at me with beautiful, mesmerizing green eyes framed with dark, full lashes. I had sisters and aunts. I noticed such things.

She had long brunette hair pulled back in a messy ponytail, soft wavy hair framing her face, and bow shaped red lips. The whole package was stunningly beautiful. So much so that I stuck my hands in my pockets to keep them from visibly trembling.

I'm not sure how many seconds passed before I realized that I was standing frozen in the middle of the ice cream parlor.

3

NOELLE

Dear Nicholas,

I've found a home here. It is nothing like where we grew up, but if nothing else, it is mine. I have an apartment above the shop where I'm working. It has a most interesting name—I won't tell you what it is right now. But oddly enough it is named after the owner's cat.

— Noelle, written to her younger brother nine months ago, after moving into her new apartment above the ice cream shop.

*M*y currently favorite Christmas song spilled from the overhead speakers. It was romantic and happy and always left me feeling good.

The murmur of voices filled in the rest of the space, surrounding me with a buffer of background noise.

This ice cream shop had become my home since I'd arrived in Whiskey Springs ten months ago. The owner, an older lady who probably by all rights, should have retired years ago, had lived in a house a few blocks away.

But when she and her husband had first opened the shop, umpteen years ago, they had built themselves a nice little one-bedroom apartment above the ice cream shop.

The shop had been a success and they had soon been able to afford a home of their own. When they moved out of the apartment upstairs, they left all the furnishings—furniture, dishes, décor.

As a result, I sometimes felt I lived in a time capsule. Even the plates I ate off of were antique. I didn't mind though. It was cozy.

Mrs. Whitman—that was her name—had used the apartment as a guest house and occasionally rented it out when the hotel overflowed, mostly in the winter.

But since I didn't have a place to stay, she allowed me to live there.

Mrs. Whitman saw something in me immediately. She never really said what it was and I never asked.

I always thought if she wanted me to know, she would tell me.

Mrs. Whitman was now living in Florida. I missed her, but even more, I missed her cat, Smedley.

A day didn't go by that some customer didn't ask about Smedley. Sometimes, they asked about Mrs. Whitman, but they always asked about Smedley.

In all the time, I had lived here in Whiskey Springs, I had not seen anyone I knew.

But today might be a different day.

The man standing frozen in the middle of my shop recognized me. I could see it in his eyes.

And I had been so very careful. So cautious.

The only person I had contacted was my brother, Nicholas, and I had sent him email from a library in Boulder.

Untraceable. And I had not told him anything that would reveal my actual location.

Using the counter for balance, I kept my gaze on his. I would not look away.

I could see now that he was tall and lean and carried himself with confidence.

Although he took three steps forward, it barely registered. One more step and I saw his eyes. Sparkling blue like the water off an island beach.

I straightened imperceptibly and lifted my chin.

Act like there is nothing wrong. Plausible deniability.

Just because he was here did not mean that he knew.

"What can I get for you?" I asked.

At first he didn't answer. I wasn't sure he even heard me.

Then he nodded toward the sign on the counter. "Can I get some of that?" he asked.

"The hot chocolate ice cream?" I asked, even though I knew exactly what he was asking for.

"Yes. Do you recommend it?"

"Of course."

He nodded once to confirm his order.

My hands trembling, I took a tall glass from the counter behind me.

"I need a place to spend the night. Do you know of any place?"

Still holding the glass, I glanced at him over my shoulder. "Did you try the saloon?" My heart was pounding like I'd just run a mile.

"The saloon has rooms?"

"Sometimes." I filled the glass halfway with hot chocolate, then proceeded to scoop up what everyone thought was miniature balls of vanilla ice cream. It wasn't actually ice cream, of course. Ice cream would melt too quickly. It was a family secret. One I had not told anyone.

In retrospect, I think the day I had introduced this to Mrs. Whitman, was the day she decided to make me manager of the ice cream shop.

As I set the glass on the counter, he laid a hundred dollar bill on the counter.

Cash. I so rarely saw cash anymore.

"I do not have change for this," I said, looking into his deep blue eyes.

He picked up the glass. "I don't need change."

"But—"

With a wave of his hand, he turned and walked back to his table.

4

GREYSON

I sat back down at my table and stared at my phone. My blank phone. And held the glass she had given me in both hands.

The girl behind the counter was not what I had expected. Not in any way. She was mid-twenties and she had a thick accent. French maybe.

She was just so much more than I had expected.

I stirred my hot chocolate with my straw. It was full of little ice cream balls. Intrigued, I used my spoon to scoop one up and pop it in my mouth.

It didn't taste like ice cream, exactly. It must be some different kind of ice cream. Maybe coated with something that kept it from melting.

A man, with his two daughters in tow, opened the door and walked outside, dusting me with a mist of cold air and jarring me out of my daze.

I googled the Whiskey Springs Saloon. Oddly enough, they didn't advertise rooms.

However, a quick phone call told me that even though they advertised rooms, they didn't have any rooms available tonight.

"Do you know of anyone in town who might have a room?" I asked.

"It's the Christmas festival," the man at the saloon said. "Rooms have been booked up for ages."

I thanked the man and hung up the phone.

My gaze was immediately drawn back to the girl behind the counter. I couldn't stop looking at her and I didn't even know her name.

I tapped my fingers on the clean table.

I would figure something out. I always did.

In the meantime, I ate all the ice cream balls out of my hot chocolate.

A message came in from Tiffany.

TIFFANY: *Are you sure you can't come home tonight? I just bought a new dress for the occasion.*

I mumbled a curse beneath my breath.

Then I answered in a more abrupt way than usual.

ME: *It wouldn't be safe. With the weather like this, I would probably crash.*

There. I'd told her how I felt and I hoped she felt remorse for valuing her dress above my life.

After watching the thought bubbles for a few seconds, I shoved my phone in my coat pocket.

I didn't have the time to worry about Tiffany right now.

I had to beat the bushes. There had to be someplace in town with a room for me to spend the night.

Sitting in the rather cramped chair at the little table, I waited while a teenage couple sampled about half a dozen ice cream flavors, then ordered a cup of vanilla and chocolate swirl.

After they paid for their order and took a seat, I stood up and stretched to my full height before walking back to the counter.

The girl, holding a white towel in her hands, watched me

warily as I approached. Her cheeks looked more flushed than I remembered.

She tilted her head to the side as I reached the counter.

"The saloon doesn't have any rooms," I said.

"Oh," she said, her brow furrowed. "That could be a problem."

"Any other ideas?"

She shook her head. Then said. "Let me make some calls."

"I don't want to cause you any trouble."

"It is no trouble." Sliding her phone out her pocket, she scrolled until she found what she was looking for.

"Watch the counter," she said. "I will be right back." Then she stepped through a door into the back.

"Watch the counter?" I repeated to myself under my breath.

I looked over my shoulder. All but a couple of the tables were filled.

What did she mean by watch the counter?

I didn't know anything about serving ice cream. And I certainly didn't know anything about make hot chocolate ice cream.

But I had to do something. She was helping me, after all.

As a boy, around twelve or so approached the counter, I nearly panicked.

Ridiculous. I flew airplanes every day. Watching the counter in an ice cream shop should most definitely not frighten me.

It should most definitely not.

And yet… somehow I was terrified.

5

NOELLE

Dear Nicholas,

I've only been here for less than three months and already I am the manager. There is so much I don't know about running a business. So much I have to learn. But I think I might be good at it. I wish you were here to share with me.

— Noelle, written to her younger brother eight months ago after being promoted to manager at the ice cream shop.

I went into the back room to make some calls. It wasn't like I knew a lot of people, but the people I did know knew people.

If there was a room to be had in Whiskey Springs, I should be able to find it.

I couldn't just leave the guy stranded.

Yes. I was taking a risk by trusting him. Possibly a huge risk. He could be looking for me.

But I wasn't going to tell him anything about myself. I wasn't going to act like someone looking for me would expect me to act.

I was going to act like any normal person would act.

And any normal person would try to help the guy find a room.

It had absolutely nothing to do with his sparkling blue eyes that sent a flutter of butterflies loose in my stomach.

Or the way his lips curved into a curious little lopsided smile when he looked at me.

And it certainly had nothing to do with the way my gaze was drawn to his lips and the way I imagined what it might be like to kiss him.

I called the Daniels House first. The Daniels House was a private house that sometimes rented rooms. The staff member who answered the phone reminded me that they were overflowing with wedding guests.

I thanked her and disconnected with a groan. I knew that.

There was no need to call the saloon. The man... Geez. I did not even know his name... had already called them.

I had one more place I could call. The Alexanders. Doc Alexander didn't have a guest room that I knew of, but he seriously knew everyone.

Of course, no one answered. Everyone was at the Festival of Trees. I left a message, then paced to the door to look out over the shop. It had become an ingrained habit. And, of course, necessary, especially when the shop was crowded like this.

"I recommend the vanilla and chocolate swirl," my new friend said.

I'd asked him to watch the counter. I hadn't expected to find him actually working *behind* the counter.

The customer was a regular and he was a difficult one. He never came in here without trying out at least three different flavors. In his defense, he usually picked one of them unlike some people who sampled a dozen flavors, then went with vanilla or chocolate.

"Okay," the boy—his name was Darryl. "I'll take that."

Wow. I was impressed. Darryl had actually gone with the vanilla chocolate swirl—without an argument.

I watched as... I really needed to get the guy's name... did an excellent job of filling a glass with the swirl of ice cream.

I smiled as he struggled with getting the top swirl done, but it wasn't half bad. Much better than my first attempt.

He set the glass on the counter. "Payment?" he asked.

Darryl held up his credit card. Then when my new helper just looked at him, Darryl explained. "You have to ring it up so I can scan it."

"Right." My new friend looked a little lost now. "Um. You know what, this one's on me. How much is it?"

Darryl looked perplexed that the checker would ask the customer for a price, but Darryl knew and to his credit, he gave an honest answer. "$4.99"

"Got it. Ah. Have a good day. Thank you for your patronage."

"Sure." Looking especially baffled now, Darryl took his ice cream and headed back to his table where he would tell his friends about his free ice cream. Or maybe about the guy behind the counter who didn't appear to know what he was doing.

Either way that could be a problem. Now everyone would want a complimentary order.

My friend pulled a five out of his money clip and looked around a moment before slipping it under the computer keyboard.

"You have experience in working in an ice cream shop?" I asked from behind him after Darryl had walked off.

"None whatsoever," he said, sliding the five dollars out and handing it to me. "Wasn't hard to figure that part out. Don't know how you take payments though."

I took the money from him, pushed a couple of keys and placed it inside the register.

"I will teach you." I glanced at Darryl's table and bit my lip. "But giving away free ice cream probably is not the best thing."

Fortunately, Darryl's friends were not overly concerned with their friend's conquest. They all had parents who gave them whatever they needed, so I could almost guarantee they weren't concerned about money anyway.

"Sorry," he said, a bit sheepishly.

"But I am impressed with your skill with the swirl. You did much better than I did on my first try."

He grinned. "Thank you for saying so. I can add it to my resume."

"Sure can," I said. "Let me know if you need a reference."

"Right now I'd settle for a room."

"I am working on that." I held out a hand. "My name is Noelle."

"I'm Greyson."

"It is a pleasure to meet you Greyson." I straightened the computer keyboard and picked up my towel to wipe the counter, although it did not need it.

I was a bit surprised that he didn't bother to go back to the other side of the counter. He seemed to be making himself at home on my side. He backed up and sat on a stool I only used on really slow days.

"What brings you to Whiskey Springs?" I asked a bit nervously. I was not prepared for him to say he was searching for me, but it seemed like the logical thing to ask. And blending in, being logical, was very important.

"Work," he said.

Work. I tamped down the bolt of alarm that shot through my system.

But then he grinned at me and my heart rate skittered.

Whether he was the one looking for me or not, I was in trouble.

I was supposed to lay low. Stay out of sight.

Not get attached.

6

_____

GREYSON

*N*oelle moved deftly as she made two milkshakes for a mother with two young children. She obviously knew what she was doing and moved with a sureness that came with experience.

I recognized the confidence that came with experience. I had it myself in the cockpit of an airplane.

Laughter from a table crowded with teens interspersed with the Christmas music streaming from the overhead speakers.

The scent of cocoa and vanilla mixed with the scent of peppermint and something else. Christmas, I decided.

Even from over here, I could smell the scent of the blue spruce.

I twirled on the little stool and looked out the window. There were a few people walking around wearing Victorian costumes.

"Is something going on in town tonight?" I asked.

Noelle washed her hands in the back counter sink and dried them on a clean cloth.

"The Christmas Festival," she said, neatly folding the towel next to the sink and turning to face me.

"What's that?" I asked.

"People, businesses mostly, decorate trees for charity. It is a contest I think."

"Your shop doesn't have a tree in it?"

She shook her head and looked out over the shop, her gaze briefly checking each table.

"I could not leave the shop."

"What about the owners? They don't have a tree?"

She tilted her head at me in that disarming way she had earlier, her expression serene, and simply shook her head.

She didn't want to say more and I wasn't inclined to push her. Not on that anyway. I had something else in mind.

"Are you the only worker tonight?" I asked, taking a little piece of peppermint from a dish on the counter. I knew the peppermint was for the ice cream shakes.

"Yes," she said, lifting a brow, but not saying anything about me eating her peppermint.

"It must be a lot for one person."

She shrugged. "It is not so much. I enjoy it."

She wasn't very talkative and the more she didn't talk, the more I wanted to know. A universal phenomenon, at least according to the most renowned psychologist in the family, Grandma Savannah.

"Where are you from?" I asked.

She hesitated and I think she almost didn't answer.

"Here and there," she said finally, looking away again.

"Military family?" I asked.

"Something like that," she said with a little smile.

I couldn't quite make out what that smile meant. To me it looked like she was keeping something to herself, but that could just be my imagination at work.

Before I could figure it out, my phone chimed.

"Do you need to take that?" she asked.

"No," I said. I knew who it was. It was Tiffany. And I wasn't in the mood for her histrionics.

The noisy group of teenagers got up and left the shop, their chairs sliding noisily across the floor. After they left, the place seemed a hundred times quieter.

"What time do you close?" I asked.

She hesitated again. Glanced at the clock behind her. "Six," she said.

That gave us a little over two hours.

"Will the Christmas tree festival still be going on?"

"I guess so." She picked up the towel again and wiped the cabinet that didn't need it.

"We'll go then," I said.

There was that hesitation. "I have to clean up."

"After the festival, we'll come back and clean up."

She set the towel down again and looked at me. "So you are just going to stay here?"

I shrugged. "I don't have anywhere else to go."

"You could go to the festival," she said.

"And what fun is that?" I asked.

She squinted at me. "You are just waiting for me to find you a room."

"Maybe," I said, grinning.

7

NOELLE

Dear Nicholas,

I have met many nice people here in Whiskey Springs. Everyone has been so welcoming. I try to answer their questions about myself—where I am from and such, but it is almost impossible without giving away my true identity.

— Noelle, written to her younger brother seven months ago after Mrs. Whitman moved to Florida, leaving her alone with the shop.

*G*reyson sat behind my counter, on the little round metal stool I inherited from Mrs. Whitman.

From all appearances, he wasn't going anywhere until after I locked up. Sometimes I closed at six and sometimes I stayed open until seven. It depended on the day. If there was no one in the shop, sometimes I just closed up. Probably lost a customer or two, but my posted closing time was six. So, I figured staying open until seven might gain a customer. At least that's what I told myself. I didn't like to admit that I did it for the company of others.

As I made one of my hot chocolate milkshakes, a recipe handed down to me by my grandmother, I watched Greyson out of the corner of my eye.

He seemed to have made himself at home and he watched me with an ease that was a little bit unsettling… in a good way.

"I've never had a hot chocolate like that," Greyson said after the customer paid and took his drinks.

I heard the question in his voice. I usually told people that it was a secret recipe that I wasn't allowed to reveal. But I felt compelled to tell Greyson the truth—or as close to the truth as I dared go.

"It's an old family recipe," I said.

"Maybe you'll tell me one day," he said.

I looked at him quickly, meeting his startling blue gaze. "Maybe," I said, trying to smile, but in that moment, ten months of loneliness fell over me like a ton of bricks.

I had done so well. I had stayed busy. Stayed to myself. And I had refused to think about the human companionship I had given up.

But now, with Greyson looking at me in that way that told me he wanted to know me—ME—not the me I was pretending to be, I heard the hint of a promise in his voice.

One day. He said. The phrase didn't mean anything. People said it every day all day long.

But I had not heard it said to me in this way in far too long.

He was saying it off-handedly, of course.

He was in Whiskey Springs on business. Hanging around, waiting for me to find a room for him.

He said he had nowhere else to be and he literally meant it. I didn't know why he was in town.

At first I'd thought he was here looking for me, but now I wasn't so sure.

Still… cautiousness was built into my DNA.

"You were planning to leave today?" I asked, turning the conversation back to him.

"That was the plan," he said, pulling out his phone, glancing at it with a frown, and putting it back in his pocket. "The client changed his mind."

I stood and just looked at him. I tried to figure out what he was truly saying while looking into his eyes.

But looking into his sparkling blue eyes was contraindicated to thinking. "The client asked you to stay over?"

"He didn't ask so much as he just decided."

"I am sorry," I said, still not understanding what it was he did. "What kind of business are you in?"

"I'm a pilot," he said.

"Oh." I stood still as a statue as I let this sink in. I mentally ran through the implications, if any, of him being a pilot.

I was well acquainted with a couple of pilots. Good men.

Greyson swept his hand down. "Guess you didn't notice the uniform," he said.

"You are wearing a coat," I said, leaning against the back cabinet. Greyson obviously wasn't going anywhere, so I might as well enjoy his company for the moment.

Not once in the ten months I'd been here had I allowed myself to indulge in any kind of conversation with a man.

It was too risky.

He grinned that lopsided grin of his that I was growing fond of much too quickly.

"I guess I am, aren't I?" He adjusted the sleeve on his woolen coat.

"You flew in to the new airport?" I asked.

He nodded.

"I hear it is very nice. Built by an investor from Texas."

"Partly," he said. "And, yes, it is a nice airport."

"You will be flying out in the morning then," I said.

"With any luck," he said, offhandedly, looking toward the front of the shop.

I blew out a sigh.

The little illusion I had been building up around him dissolved like the little bubbles I had played with as a child.

He might be here now—tonight—but he was ready to get back to his life.

And I was not part of that life.

8

GREYSON

I was not one of those guys. A girl in every port and all that.

My motto was *flight attendants are not a dating pool.*

I had stolen the motto from my Aunt Madison, a university professor. She had been complaining about faculty having relationships with students. *Students are not a dating pool,* she insisted.

Of course, Aunt Madison, happily married to Uncle Kade, had never been in such a situation. She'd met Kade in college. It had taken a few years for them to make it stick, or so the story went, but now they were inseparable.

So sitting here on the little metal stool—all the furniture in this shop was a tad bit too small for me—I tried to analyze why I was hanging around Noelle.

It wasn't loneliness. I actually enjoyed my time alone whenever I had to go on an overnight trip. I explored some, then usually headed back to my room for a glass of wine, a movie, and sometimes a good book. I did not require a lot of entertainment.

If I wanted drama, all I had to do was talk to Tiffany.

And yet here I was, unwilling to pull myself away from Noelle's company.

It was, of course, simply because she had agreed to ask around for a room for me for tonight.

I had never been in a situation where I couldn't find a room somewhere. I had spent the night at a client's house once and that was my safety net for tonight. If I couldn't find a place, I was not above calling Mr. Williams, my client, and letting him know that I needed a bed for the night.

He should, in fact, have offered, but he seemed distracted by whatever it was he was doing. So I would leave that option as a last resort.

Besides, I was enjoying Noelle, even though I seemed to make her a bit uncomfortable.

She needn't worry about me. I was an upstanding guy. She had no way of knowing that, though. She wasn't from here, so she wouldn't know my connection with the *investor from Texas* who had something to do with building the airport.

I wasn't sure she would put it all together even if I told her my last name.

She seemed a bit like a fish out of water. A fish who was trying very hard to keep up the appearance of being in the water.

I had to be honest with myself and admit that I really wanted to figure her out. I wanted that more than I wanted to find a room.

It just so happened that, at the moment at least, the two fit hand in hand.

Two of the other tables emptied out. Everyone, it seemed, was heading to the Christmas Tree festival.

"Do you think everyone is going to the tree festival?" I asked, putting voice to my question.

She shrugged a little. "I do not really know."

"Is it usually crowded?"

"I do not know," she said again. "This is my first Christmas here."

"Are you here with family?" I'd already checked, but I glanced at her bare ring finger again.

"Uh-uh," she said, with a little shake of her head.

"Then how did you end up here?"

"I read about it," she said somewhat hesitantly. "And wanted to visit."

"But… you stayed."

"I stayed," she said, her gaze meeting mine for a moment, before skittering away.

There was something she wasn't telling me.

Another customer left the shop, leaving only two occupied tables.

I glanced at the time. It was pushing five o'clock.

"We should head out to the festival now," I said.

With a little alarm, she glanced out at the customer area. "There are still people here," she said, keeping her voice low.

"Maybe it's time for them to leave," I said, standing up and walking out from behind the counter.

"Wait," she said.

But I was already on a mission. I stopped halfway between the two tables. They were all finished eating, just sitting and talking.

"So," I said, with one of my smiles that usually won people over. "We're about to close and head over to the Tree Festival. Thought you all might to go, too."

And within minutes, I had them up and out the door.

Once they were out, I turned the little sign to closed, and locked the door.

Feeling quite proud of my achievement, I turned and grinned back at Noelle.

But she was standing there with her hands on her hips, her brow furrowed.

Maybe… just maybe… I should have checked with her first.

9

NOELLE

Dear Nicholas,

I never thought I would enjoy hard work so much. Ha. Ha. I get up early, go to work, then spend my evenings winding down. Everyone says I should hire someone to help me in the shop, but I enjoy making all the decisions. Doing everything myself. I know... you must think this whole thing is so foreign and unlike me.

— Noelle, written to her younger brother six months ago during the height of the busy summer tourist season in Whiskey Springs.

I should be mad at Greyson, at least that's what I thought I should be.

But he looked so proud of himself, standing there, grinning at me.

He'd gotten my last two customers—in his defense, they were just lingering anyway—out the door, thinking it was their idea. Did he not remember that he, too, was a lingerer? He'd sat alone at the table nearest the door for some time before he decided he should buy something.

"We can go now," he said, sheepishly.

I could see him as a little boy, caught with his hand in the cookie jar, feeling so proud of himself for his success, but knowing that he had done something he wasn't supposed to do.

I ducked into the back room where the big freezers and the boxes of supplies were along with the big commercial dishwasher, mostly to hide the smile that tugged at my lips, no matter how hard I tried to keep from smiling.

Grabbing my long woolen coat from the little coat closet, I shrugged into it. Added a scarf and gloves. I hadn't even checked the weather lately. But it wasn't snowing and people were moving about, walking up and down the sidewalk so it must be tolerable.

It went against everything in me to leave the shop in such disarray—dirty glasses sitting on the tables, chairs all askew, but I turned off the light and walked toward Greyson.

He was waiting for me next to the door, a charcoal gray scarf now wrapped around his neck.

I tried to keep my expression stern, but when he grinned at me, even biting my lip couldn't keep my own smile at bay.

When he held out his arm, I put my hand in the crook of his elbow and followed him out the door.

The brisk cold wind shocked my senses as it struck my face, the only place I had that was unprotected.

Greyson did not seem to be the least bit affected. If anything, the cold put a pep in his step.

His enthusiasm was contagious.

As we walked along the sidewalk, bursting with joyful Christmas tunes, twinkling with bright red and green lights, I felt a lightness in my heart that I hadn't felt in such a long time. Too long to even think about.

"Hello," Abby, one of the first-grade teachers from the elementary school greeted us at the door. I recognized her from when she had come into the shop with a group of students. I remembered her due to her distinctive highlighted blonde hair. The students all loved her, even if it was just because they love looking at her. She reminded me of a Barbie doll.

Today, she was wearing one of the Victorian costumes—a long dress and a little bonnet that harked back to centuries gone past.

"You're just in time for the voting." She handed me a ballot and a small wooden half-pencil with no eraser.

"And one for your boyfriend," she said as she handed an identical ballot and pencil to Greyson.

"He's not—"

"Thank you," Greyson said, his words drowning out mine as he pulled me away from Abby and the door.

The high school gym was crowded. A dozen festively decorated blue spruce trees lined the perimeter while people— some bundled up like us and others wearing Victorian costumes—walked around, most holding ballots, just as we were.

"What was that?" I asked, once we were out of earshot.

"The first rule of being a good companion," he said. "Never let people think you're available."

"Why?" I asked, my voice trailing off as I looked over my shoulder toward the door where Abby stood.

She was looked our way. Or rather, to be exact, she was clearly staring at Greyson.

"Oh," I said, looking back at him. He, on the other hand, had his attention focused on the nearest tree decorated in white owls and blue ribbons. "I see what you mean."

Seemingly unconcerned, he looked down at his ballot. "Tree number one is surprisingly fetching, don't you think?"

"Fetching?" I asked, choosing to focus on his odd choice of word instead of his odd taste in Christmas trees.

He leaned over and said in a stage whisper. "We're among the Victorians."

I put a hand over my mouth to keep from laughing out loud.

"Indeed," I said. "I think we might be underdressed."

"I don't think anyone notices. We're like specters," he said. "Just wandering among the earth-bound commoners."

I looked at him sideways. If only he knew how close he was to the truth. "Specters as in ghosts or spies?"

He looked at me with surprise.

It occurred to me then that he actually saw me as who I portrayed myself to be. He saw me as a girl who worked in an ice cream parlor. He didn't see me as the owner and he certainly didn't sense my true identity.

"A little of both," he said, patting my gloved hand with his gloved hand. "Ghost spies here to seek out the best Christmas tree in Whiskey Springs." He paused a moment. "Except of course for the one at the ice cream parlor. That one stands above all other trees in the town."

"There's no need to flatter me," I said. "I know the truth.

He was looking at me now with curiosity.

"The truth, eh?"

"Yes," I said with a definitive nod. "The truth."

"Perhaps you'll share this truth with me."

"Perhaps I will," I said, stopping to admire the second tree on our path. "One day."

10

GREYSON

I was enjoying myself immensely.

I would, of course, have to vehemently deny that to any of my family, should it ever be discovered. Walking around looking for the best decorated Christmas trees with a girl whose name I barely knew on my arm, they would never let me live it down.

But since I was stuck here in the little Christmas town of Whiskey Springs for the evening, I thought I might as well enjoy myself.

Normally, I would treat myself to a nice local dinner, maybe get a burger and fries with a beer. Then I'd spend the rest of the evening walking around, taking in the ambiance of the place before turning in early.

Since I would never have more than one beer—half a beer, truth be known—since I had to fly the next day. Twelve hours bottle to throttle. And never more than one. I had developed a habit of having quiet evenings. I'd known too many pilots who developed bad habits of trolling bars and women when they were out of town on flights.

My Grandpa, Noah Worthington, expected better of his

pilots, and certainly better of his children and grandchildren. And he got it.

The thought of having to explain to Grandpa Noah how I got myself into trouble struck fear into my heart. I would sooner have the ground open up and swallow me whole.

But this Christmas Tree festival with Noelle was the complete opposite of trouble. I was here milling about with the upstanding people of Whiskey Springs.

No one could ask for more.

The fact that I was enjoying myself probably shocked me more than anyone, although it shouldn't. I had sisters. I could spend the day at the mall with the best of them. And I made it a point to always enjoy myself no matter if I was doing something I enjoyed or if I was doing something someone I cared about enjoyed doing.

"What's the second rule?" Noelle asked as we dodged our way to the next tree.

"What?" Confused, I looked over at her. Her head was tilted to the side as she studied a tree decorated with an odd combination of yellow and white decorations. So odd that it distracted me from her question. "What do you think they're trying to portray here?" I asked, looking up at the tree.

"I don't know," Noelle said. "Maybe a sunrise or a sunset?"

"Maybe," I said, but there was something disconcerting about it. Like eating canned green beans. I shuddered and looked away.

Without even having to say anything else, we turned and walked to the next tree. "So what's the second rule?" she asked again, since I had yet to answer her.

"Rule about what?" I marked through the yellow and white tree, eliminating it from my list of possible winners.

"You said there were rules of being a good companion. Rules. Plural."

"Right. I did, didn't I?"

We stopped at the next tree, decorated all in blue. Blue ribbons. Blue lights. Blue ornaments. It had an icy cold feel to it. I liked it.

"Yes," she said, keeping her gaze on me. "You did."

I grinned over at her. "I have to give that some thought."

"So there aren't any other rules?"

"There are other rules," I said. "I just have to remember them. Do you like this tree?"

She hesitated, still staring at me, then turned and studied the blue tree. "I like it," she said.

"Me too," I said, putting a little arrow next to it. "The first thing we have to do is eliminate the ones we don't like. Then we can go back and rank the ones we do like."

"You're really getting into this," she said, her gaze moving from my ballot back to my eyes.

"I get into everything I do," I said and grinned to myself at her fetching blush.

11

NOELLE

Dear Nicholas,

I know you warned me about this. And I knew you were right. But experiencing the loneliness of being, well... alone in a strange place sometimes takes my breath away. I almost caved in and called you. But I stuck to my plan.

— Noelle, written to her younger brother five months ago after having to be sequestered in her apartment with a terrible stomach bug for two days.

*a*fter Greyson and I had walked around the gym and looked at all the trees, we sat on a little bench and compared notes.

We had each earmarked three trees that we liked.

We both liked the one decorated in solid blue.

And we both liked the one decorated in a traditional

manner with red and silver balls. It was very sedate and reminded me of the Christmas trees from home.

He liked the one with the white owls and blue ribbons, although I didn't see the allure of it that he saw. He also liked the one with the steam engine trains. I understood how he liked that one, since he was a guy and it was definitely a guy's tree.

I also liked the one decorated in an ombre style. The balls started with pink at the base, going through shades of blue and green, culminating with gold balls at the top.

I tapped what served as a pencil against my paper. "If we don't vote together," I said. "we cancel each other out."

He was grinning at me again, even though I was scowling at him.

I wondered if he had gotten through his life using that smile as his secret weapon. If he had, I could see how it worked.

I glanced toward the door where Abby still stood. And even in that brief glance, I caught her staring at Greyson. She looked away quickly, but it was too late. She was busted.

Then I saw another young lady walk by, her gaze also stayed longer than necessary on Greyson.

I shifted my gaze over to him. His attention was on his ballot, with glances at the decorated trees. He seemed to be completely unaware that he was the center of attention with the ladies.

"You're right," he said, turning to me and locking his eyes on mine.

As I gazed into his eyes, unable to look away—indeed, why would I want to—my breath hitched, just a little. His eyes were blue, but not just blue. I was close enough to see that they had little almost imperceptible streaks of deep green.

But it wasn't just the color. It was the way his eyes smiled. I watched people, so I knew that when a lot of people smiled, their smile did not reach their eyes. Fake smiles. Maybe not fake, but not real like Greyson's.

"I am right about what?" I asked.

"We should vote together."

"Okay," I said. And in that moment, if he had wanted me to vote for that horrid yellow and white tree, I would have done so.

Fortunately, he didn't ask me to do that.

"Are you favoring the blue one, the classic one, or the ombre one?"

I glanced at his paper. "The ombre one is not on your list," I pointed out.

He shrugged. "Okay. Blue or classic?"

I looked past the people milling about and scanned the trees. "The blue, I think."

"Blue it is, then," he said and put a check mark next to the blue one. Tree number five.

I nodded and did the same.

He held up a hand, palm out. I placed my own palm against his. But instead of merely tapping hands, as I had expected, he linked his fingers with mine.

"We are a good team," he said.

I nodded, since I was having trouble thinking. His hand on mine was so unexpected. So… real… so… everything.

12

GREYSON

*T*he high school gym was crowded with so many different people. It was an odd mix.

Most people, of course, were dressed in regular clothes like us. There were a few people wearing Victorian costumes—long dresses, bonnets, and scarves. Wearing Victorian costumes at Christmastime was something new, to me at least.

There were also children running around excitedly, having a grand time. Most of the mothers had given up trying to keep a rein on them. Christmas was for children, after all. If anyone should be enjoying themselves, it should be the children.

I don't know what happened when I held up my hand for a high-five. I really had no control over my fingers as they clasped hers.

It was like they were magnetized. I didn't want to let go, but somehow, through Herculean strength, I did.

Noelle showed no response other than a widening of her eyes.

They were green, but not just green. They had shards of light green, dark green, brown, and even a hint of blue. They were mesmerizing. Pulling me toward the rocks where I would be lost forever.

"Shall we turn in our ballots?" I asked.

"Yes," she said, straightening and running her hands along her thighs.

Together, we made our way toward the ballot box up front, near the door.

The woman who had handed us our ballots was still there and she was doing everything she could to catch my attention.

I had no interest in her. I didn't even need to know her name.

We slid our ballots into the box.

"That's done," I said, putting my hands on my hips. "Now what happens?"

"I guess that is it. At least until all the votes are counted."

"That could take hours," I said. "Want to get something to eat?"

"Sure," she said, her lips curving in that way that I found to be irresistible.

"Is there a burger place near here?"

She hesitated, bit her lip, as she stuffed her hands into her coat. "There is a place called the Hungry Hat," she said. "I think they have hamburgers."

I found it curious that she did not seem to know for sure.

"We can walk?" I asked.

"Of course." She turned toward the door.

I pushed the door open and held it for her to walk through. The wind whipped her hair, tossing it back over her shoulders.

It had gotten cold while we were inside.

Clouds hovered over the rugged Rocky Mountain peaks in the distance. Snow. It was snowing in the high country.

Christmas was just days, three days, away. I wondered if it would be snowing here for Christmas.

I held out my arm for Noelle. As she'd done before, she tucked her hand in the crook of my elbow.

If I didn't get to fly soon... tomorrow, I could be snowed in.

I'd never missed a Christmas with my family. The Worthington clan was close. My mother, Brianna Worthington, by birth, had instilled in her five children a strong, close bond emphasizing family. *Friends will come and go, she said, but family will always be there.*

As I walked along the streets of Whiskey Springs toward a place called the Hungry Hat, Christmas music streaming over hidden speakers, twinkling Christmas lights sparkling all around us as the sun began to drop below the mountains, I found myself with an unexpected thought.

I found myself wishing for snow. Lots of snow. Snow that covered everything and shut everything down. Including airports.

We turned down a side street, heading toward the noisy, crowded restaurant called The Hungry Hat. People stood around, huddled in the cold, sat on benches, waiting for a table.

We stepped inside the door where it was even more crowded inside than it was outside and were told that there was an hour's wait.

I took the old-fashioned pager—hadn't seen one of those in a long time—and turned away, Noelle at my side.

"Is it worth it?" I asked. "The wait?"

"I do not know." She shrugged. "I have never eaten here."

Whiskey Springs was not a big town. As far as towns went, it was quite small. It wasn't like there were a ton of restaurants to eat at here.

My heart went out to her. That she lived here and had never even eaten at one of the few restaurants in town. The girl was a mystery. And I felt sorry for her.

I could not help thinking that something was not quite right.

And on the heels of that thought, came another.

Perhaps I was the one to make things right for her.

13

NOELLE

Dear Nicholas,

Today, I thought I recognized someone from home. Our language tutor from years ago. I haven't thought about him in ages, but it was such a startling sensation. I was unsettled for the rest of the day.

— Noelle, written to her younger brother four months ago after she thought she saw her language tutor looking inside her shop window.

The hour to get a table at the Hungry Hat turned in one and a half hours.

I didn't really know what to expect about whether the food was good or not. But it certainly smelled good and the line out the door to get in suggested that it was worth the wait.

Of course, I didn't recognize any of the people waiting, so most of them had to be tourists. They probably didn't know whether the food was good either. Besides, the saloon, downtown, this was supposed to be one of the best restaurants in town, so it surely couldn't be all that bad.

We ordered glasses of Rosé wine and found a private little bench to sit on between the gas fireplace and the large festive blue spruce Christmas tree.

It was a small bench, probably meant for one person, but we both managed to sit, side by side, on it. Being pressed this close up against Greyson was a little disconcerting, but it also felt right and safe.

I tried not to think about it. Instead I tried to focus on the comforting scent of French fries and hamburgers mixed with the strong bough of the spruce tree against my shoulder.

"How would you rate this one?" I asked, looking at the Christmas tree next to me. It was probably the most simply decorated tree we had seen all day. Just decked out in silver and gold ribbons, beads, and balls with a big festive silver and gold bow on the very top.

Greyson glanced over at it. Nodded. "I think it looks like a tree fit for a princess."

I froze, my wine glass a mere inch from my lips.

I blinked and watched him out of the corner of my eyes. But my hands were trembling. I quickly set the glass down and held my hands together in my lap.

What an odd choice of words he had used to describe the tree.

I agreed that the decorations were elegant and simple. This tree, although smaller, was similar in appearance to the ones I had grown up with.

Greyson didn't seem to notice that he had said anything out of the ordinary. That he'd said anything I might find alarming.

As I was still processing what he'd said, our pager lit up, indicating that our table was ready.

He quickly stood up and held out a hand to help me up.

As I put my hand in his and he led me toward our table, I was distracted away from our discussion of the tree.

I let out a breath. It had just been a figure of speech. That was all.

As we settled in at our table, I noticed that Greyson had barely touched his wine.

I hadn't either, but I rarely drank, especially when I was trying to keep my wits about me. And being out in public it was necessary to stay alert.

"You don't like your wine?" I asked.

"I like it fine," he said. "It's just a bottle to throttle thing."

The server came by to hand us menus and glasses of water.

"A what?" I asked, after the server had walked off.

"Bottle to throttle," he said again. "A pilot has to have all his wits about him. I have to be alert for my flight in the morning."

"Right," I said, turning my own glass gently by the stem as I watch the pale pink liquid swirling in the glass.

He was thinking about flying out tomorrow, not thinking about me at all.

I needed to pull myself together.

To recognize this for what it was.

Just one night.

14

GREYSON

*T*he restaurant was crowded with all sorts of people. I heard a few different accents, mostly locals, I decided, but some tourists, too.

It was loud and there was that excitement in the air that was only there around the holidays. It would be great if Christmas came at least twice a year. Might lose some of its magic, though. Probably.

I liked the loudness of the restaurant that spilled around us. I liked the way it seemed to wrap a bubble around Noelle and me. I could hear her perfectly as the other voices were merely background.

I didn't recognize anyone from the Tree Festival. Not that I would, necessarily. I certainly didn't see anyone dressed in Victorian costume.

The server brought a basket of chips and two little cups of salsa.

Noelle was jumpy.

I wasn't sure exactly what I'd said that had started it. I think we'd been talking about the Christmas tree we'd been sitting next to, but that made no sense. We'd been looking at and talking about trees all afternoon.

Whatever it was, I wanted it to go away. I wanted to get back to the easy companionship we'd had during our time at the Tree Festival.

Maybe we'd walk back by there and find out who won the contest. I was curious. We'd spent a good deal of time studying the different trees and oddly enough, we had come to an agreement on which one was the best.

It had to win. There was no way both of us could be wrong.

I hadn't really planned to vote for the one with the battery-operated steam engine trains, but I'd found it fascinating in its uniqueness. Someone had most definitely outdone themselves with their creativity.

My phone chimed again while we waited for our food. I didn't hear it so much as I felt it vibrate.

It was probably Tiffany, but I couldn't be sure. It might be my client or it might be someone in my family looking for me.

They were used to not being able to get in touch with me when I was flying, but when I wasn't flying they knew they could contact me and I would respond.

I pulled the phone out of my pocket and glanced at the message.

Tiffany.

I seriously thought she would have given up by now. She seemed to have some kind of radar that told her I was out with someone else. Not that she and I were exclusive. We weren't even really dating.

And this wasn't a date... exactly. Although, I thought, with a glance over at Noelle. She was watching over the glass of wine that she was pretending to drink.

Felt like a date.

"Do you need to get that?" she asked.

"Probably," I said. "Eventually. But it's not something that can't wait."

"Girlfriend?" she asked.

I nearly dropped the chip I was about to dip into the salsa.

"Friend," I said.

"Ah," she said with a raised eyebrow. She set her glass down. Fidgeted with her napkin. There was another question coming. I knew it was.

"Does she know that?"

I laughed. "Good question," I said. "Maybe not."

She glanced over her shoulder. "Maybe she is tracking you with your phone."

"What?" I glanced down in the general direction of my phone, then looked back up into her eyes.

She just smiled and shrugged a little, but didn't say anything else.

"I don't know," I said. I'd never given it any thought. I'd had no reason to. Tiffany and I were not exclusive. She had no reason to know my whereabouts.

I found myself looking over my shoulder as well. Of course, I knew, there was no way for Tiffany to even need to know where I was. She shouldn't even care. I'd told her I couldn't make it back to Houston tonight. And that was that.

"I'll just turn this thing off," I said and proceeded to do just that. In that remote event that she could actually track me, turning off my phone would put a stop to that, wouldn't it?

I had more important things to worry about. Like where I was going to sleep tonight.

And, perhaps even more importantly, what I was going to do about my attraction to Noelle.

15

NOELLE

Dear Nicholas,

I wish you were here. The season's first snowflakes of autumn today. Such soft, fluffy flakes. It reminded me so much of home. It was beautiful.

— Noelle, written to her younger brother three months ago after the first snowfall in Whiskey Springs.

The food at the Hungry Hat was surprisingly good. I rarely ate this kind of food. Hamburgers and French fries were not on my regular diet. Maybe it was because I was starving. I think I had forgotten to eat lunch. That happened sometimes when I was busy.

When I got back from the restroom, Greyson had already paid the server.

"Ready?" he asked, standing up as I reached the table.

"We have to pay," I said.

"It's taken care of." He held up my coat while I slipped my arms into it.

I started to protest, but I decided it wasn't worth it.

I still needed to find him a place to stay tonight. As we walked toward the door, I checked my phone. I had no messages.

That meant that Greyson had no place to sleep tonight.

My contacts, such as they were, had not come through.

I needed to think.

There had to be something.

"Everything okay?" Greyson asked as we stepped outside.

It was twilight. That beautiful time of day when only the last remnants of sunlight remained and the chilly blanket of cold was settling into the valley for the night.

"Uh-huh," I said, pulling my scarf tighter around me and keeping my gaze from his.

My mind was racing. I should have already followed up about a room for him.

"Something seems to be bothering you," he said.

"I just need to call someone," I said. "I need to find you a place to stay for the night."

"No responses then?"

"Not yet. Everyone is at the festival, I guess." Although I knew it wasn't true. No one called me back because they were doing something else. I hadn't seen Mrs. Alexander at the festival. If I had, I would have asked her directly if she knew anyone who might have a room to let for the night.

I was getting a little nervous about it.

We walked by the gym, but the doors were already locked, the lights off.

"I guess we won't know who won," Greyson said.

"Oh," I said. "We'll know. It will be in the newspaper."

"There's a newspaper?" he asked, looking at me as though I'd sprouted an extra head.

"Of course," I said, with a little grin as I looked up at him from beneath my lashes. Then I added. "It will be on the Internet, too."

"Whiskey Springs is caught between the past and the present."

I glanced up at him sideways. "That's an interesting way to sum it up."

We reached my shop and after I unlocked the door, we stepped into the warmth.

But then I was immediately reminded that I had left everything in complete disarray.

I stood in the middle of the shop and looked around with dismay. I needed to clean it all up, but first I had to find Greyson a place to stay the night.

I didn't know what I was going to do, but I did know one thing.

He couldn't stay with me.

16

GREYSON

*N*oelle went into the back room to make some phone calls. I admired her determination to find me a place to stay the night.

I could still call Mr. Williams, but if I was going to do it, I needed to do it sooner rather than later.

But first, I needed to give Noelle time to find me something. I didn't want her to think she'd been wasting her time all along.

The shop itself was a mess. There were half-full glasses of melted ice cream on the tables and dirty napkins scattered about. The tables were in complete disarray.

I'd never worked in a restaurant, but sometimes being a pilot meant essentially being a server. Most people didn't think about that, but private pilots don't have flight attendants. The pilot is not only the driver, but also the flight attendant.

So I was used to serving people. Cleaning up, not so much. Skye Travels had a cleaning crew that came in and cleaned the planes between passengers.

But I could do cleaning, too. My parents had raised us to know how to take care of ourselves and we had daily chores.

I pulled off my woolen coat and draped it over the back of a chair. Then pulled off my suit jacket. Draped it over the chair, too.

The least I could do for Noelle was to help her out. I had been the one, after all, who had insisted that she go with me to the festival.

I didn't know if she had to work in the morning or not, but either way, I would not be the one getting her in trouble with her boss.

So I rolled up my sleeves above my elbows and got busy.

While I worked, I found myself thinking about Noelle. Which led me to thoughts of Tiffany.

I needed to do something about Tiffany.

It was time for that *relationship of convenience* to end. The way she was texting and even calling today was too much of an overreaction. Even for her. I was used to her drama. Maybe I just hadn't paid it all that much attention until this particular moment. Today.

It had been some time since I had paid more than passing romantic attention to a girl other than Tiffany. I kept myself above board, focusing mostly on family and work.

But now that I'd met Noelle and spent time with her, I was realizing just how much I had been missing. I didn't regret missing out because missing out until now left me open and available to meeting Noelle.

She was a mystery, but a mystery that I was intensely enjoying solving.

I filled the sink with soapy water, dunked a cloth into it and went to the table closest to the window. I'd start there and work my way back to the counter.

I quickly got into a routine and found myself whistling some inane tune while I worked. I was enjoying the companionableness of it all. Of being here with Noelle.

I could hear Noelle talking in the back room. At least someone must have answered her phone.

I figured if Noelle didn't find anything and Mr. Williams didn't come through, I could sleep right here on the floor of the ice cream shop. With a quick glance at my watch, I wondered if I had time to run to the general store to grab a blanket and a pillow.

Maybe Noelle had extras.

I could escort her home, then bring back what I needed. If she would trust me with her keys. Surely she would. I'd never had any trouble with people trusting me.

I had to be careful though. There was no way I was going to spend the night at her place.

First of all, it would not be proper.

And second of all, I just didn't trust myself to be that close to her.

Being that close to her would only make me want to kiss her.

And since the weather was not cooperating, it looked like I would be flying out tomorrow.

It didn't matter that my grandfather was a major investor in the airport here. He was a major investor in a lot of things in a lot of places.

I couldn't predict when I would be back here.

No. It was not a good idea to get too attached to Noelle.

It would be most ungentlemanly to kiss a girl and leave.

17

NOELLE

Dear Nicholas,

You will never believe what has happened. Mrs. Whitman has given me the ice cream shop. Truly. My name is on the deed. I own an ice cream shop in Whiskey Springs. I did not set out to own anything here. I have a lot of responsibility now. I have to make sure I do it justice.

— Noelle, written to her younger brother two months ago after Mrs. Whitman deeded the ice cream shop to her.

I had spoken to everyone I knew to talk to and I had come up empty. I hadn't found a place for Greyson to spend the night. I had come up empty handed.

Struggling to figure out something to tell him—some consolation, I stepped from the back into the shop and my breath hitched as I took in the scene.

The ice cream shop was sparkling clean, all the chairs

pushed neatly up to the tables. Everything in its place. All the debris and dirty glasses picked up and hidden away.

Greyson stood at the sink, the sleeves of his white button down shirt rolled up, his arms up to his elbows in soapy water. He was whistling something as he stood there washing glasses.

He didn't see me. I stood there. Just admiring the man. He was about six feet tall. Lean. And held himself with confidence.

He was a pilot, but here he was standing in my ice cream shop washing dishes.

As a pilot, this wasn't something he would be accustomed to doing.

That meant that both of us, unbeknownst to him, were operating outside our usual activities.

He must have felt me watching him. He turned and grinned, a little sheepishly. I saw the little boy that he must have been— caught doing something he probably wasn't supposed to be doing.

I smiled back. It was really all I could do.

"I'm almost finished," he said.

"Would you like some help?" I asked, biting my lip. It wouldn't be nice to tell him that I had a dishwasher in the back.

"Would you mind checking the forecast?" he asked.

"Sure." That was not at all what I expected him to ask me to do.

I opened the weather app on my phone and scrolled through. "Tonight? Or tomorrow?"

"Both."

"Tonight is clear with temperatures in the thirties."

"Tomorrow?"

"Clear with temperatures in low forties."

He rinsed his hands and dried them. "Even the weather conspires against me today."

"What's that?" I asked, looking up at him, not understanding.

"Nothing," he said, shaking his head. "Any luck on a room?"

I shook my head. "I'm not sure what to do now."

He shrugged. "It's no big deal. I'll walk you home, then, if it's okay with you, I can bring back a blanket and sleep here."

"Sleep where?" I pictured him sleeping on chairs, but that would never work.

"On the floor."

"You can't sleep on the floor," I said.

He gazed at me a moment and I wondered what, exactly, he could possibly be thinking.

"It's getting late. I should walk you home."

I felt a little panic wash over me. I had no reason to panic. It wasn't logical.

And yet…

He rolled down his sleeves and buttoned the cuffs, then grabbed up his jacket while I stood frozen.

Then he seemed to notice that I had not moved. "Is there something else we need to do?" he said as he quickly scanned the room.

I shook my head, then found my voice. "Everything is fine. There's nothing else."

"Come on, then," he said, picking up his coat. "I'll walk you home."

"You can't.

His expression changed. He looked startled. "You're… with someone?"

"No," I said quickly. "It's just that." I took a deep breath and just spit it out. "I live here."

18

GREYSON

*N*oelle stood in the middle of the shop, watching me, not making any moves to get her coat.

Her dark hair framed her perfectly heart shaped face. She watched me with sparkling green eyes, but it was those lips, those perfectly bow shaped red lips that sent my blood rushing through my veins.

Noelle was almost heartbreakingly beautiful and I had trouble pulling my eyes away from her.

In the back of my mind, I wondered, what was such a beautiful young lady doing here, working in an ice cream shop in this little town of Whiskey Springs? She could be anywhere doing anything she wanted to.

One day someone was going to walk in here and sweep her off her feet. Someone was going to take her away from here.

That thought was oddly disturbing, so much so that I had use the nearest red chair to steady myself, my woolen coat still draped over my arm.

I smelled like dish soap, but it was worth it. The little shop sparkled, giving me a sense of achievement. Everything was clean and orderly. The shop was ready to open in the morning.

There were probably other things she had to do that I didn't know about, but it was a sight better than it had been when we had arrived.

For a moment, all the hopes and dreams I hadn't even known I had crashed around me as it suddenly occurred to me she might have a boyfriend or even, God forbid, a husband.

I should never have made assumptions.

But it wasn't that at all.

"You live here?" I looked around the ice cream shop. Surely this was some kind of jest. People often said they lived at their place of work, but they didn't *literally* mean it.

"Yes," she said.

"But where do you sleep?" I looked at her sideways, waiting for her to tell me that she was merely being funny.

"Upstairs," she said. "My apartment is upstairs."

"Oh. I see."

Well. That made things a bit more complicated, didn't it? I didn't have to walk her home. She was already home.

"Then do you mind if I sleep on the floor?"

She laughed a little. "I can't let you sleep on the floor."

I shrugged. Didn't seem a lot different from sleeping in an airport to me. Although people did it all the time, I had only had to do it once. But since I had done it that one time, I knew I could. That was the way of things wasn't it? Once a person had done something, they could do it again and it was almost always much easier over time.

She put her hands on her hips and seemed to study me. It felt like she was looking for an answer to a question only she knew.

"You will sleep on my sofa," she announced, as though she had suddenly made a decision and there would be no more questions.

I couldn't explain my mixed emotions at that moment. I felt

a jolt of happiness, but I reflexively tamped it down, replacing it with a resounding resistance.

Hadn't I just lectured myself on how improper it would be for me to spend the night in her vicinity?

Especially since I already knew that I wanted to kiss her.

And the weather was not cooperating in the least. I would be flying out tomorrow. I was certain of it.

I couldn't kiss this girl and fly away not knowing when I would see her again. I had already crossed my own line in the sand by spending the afternoon with her.

And yet... I was drawn to her. And if she wanted me to sleep on her sofa, I was pretty sure that was exactly what I was going to be doing.

19

NOELLE

Dear Nicholas,

Today I did something you would not believe. I admit I had a little—a lot—of help with delivery, but I picked out a live blue spruce Christmas tree and decorated it. It wasn't such a big deal, but I did it all by myself. I feel more confident. I feel like I really can do this. And I'm not the least bit lonely.

— Noelle, written to her younger brother one month ago after she bought and decorated her own Christmas tree

*G*reyson followed me through the storage room to the stairs that led up to my apartment. There was also a stairway at the back outside, but, of course, I had no need to use it. I had, in fact, placed a desk in front of it, giving me a breathtaking view of the rugged rocky mountain peaks.

Although I never had guests, I kept my apartment clean and

tidy. I didn't own a lot of things, so I didn't have a lot to keep up with.

All the furnishings had been here since I had moved in. The sofa was a bit threadbare, but it still served its purpose.

I had spent countless hours sitting there, mostly reading. Like the rest of the furniture, it had its share of snags and scratch marks from the cat the ice cream shop was named after, Smedley. It didn't bother me in the least. I considered it part of the charm of the place and, in some way, it made me feel like the cat was still around.

Like everyone else, I still missed Smedley being here—he used to come up and curl up with me on the sofa, but from all accounts from Mrs. Whitman, he was enjoying the Florida sunshine. Mrs. Whitman reported that he even had his own window seat to catch the morning rays.

I reached the top of the stairs, Greyson on my heels, and flipped on the light switch.

"This is it," I said, thankful for my habit of keeping everything neat and tidy. "This is my apartment."

"If you have an extra blanket," he said for about the fourth time, "I can just sleep on the floor downstairs."

I put a hand on the sofa. "I have blankets, but you can sleep here."

I couldn't have Greyson sleeping on the floor. Somehow during the course of the day, he had become my friend.

In another place and time, perhaps he could have been more than a friend.

But he was only here for a short time and I... well... I... wasn't in a position to put down roots either.

I hadn't meant to own an ice cream shop. It had come about accidently.

An ice cream shop was one thing. Being attached to a person was another thing entirely.

"Okay," he said. "I'll sleep on your sofa."

He made it sound like such a concession that it made me smile.

"I'll get you a blanket," I said. "and a pillow."

Going to my linen closet, I pulled out a blanket and a pillow. They smelled a little musty—I'd never used them and they had been here when I moved in. But there was nothing to be done about it. A man who was willing to sleep on the floor, couldn't be too picky about a little musty smell on his linens.

By the time I came back to the living room, Greyson was lounging on the sofa, his long legs stretched out in front of him, his hands clasped in his lap.

His eyes were closed.

I envied him.

I envied that he could be so relaxed without a care in the world. So relaxed that he could sit on a stranger's sofa and simply fall asleep.

But the minute I took a step in his direction, he opened his eyes and smiled at me with a lazy smile.

I swallowed thickly, feeling attraction for him down to my toes.

"I have your blankets and pillow," I said, unnecessarily, laying them on one end of the sofa.

"You're very kind," he said.

I just shrugged. "Do you need anything else?"

His eyes locked onto mine and neither one of us looked away for several seconds that surely melded into at least a full minute.

I was suddenly bone-weary tired.

It was a big sofa, big enough for both of us. I dropped onto the opposite end from where he sat.

Following his example, I leaned back and closed my eyes.

Neither one of us said anything for a few minutes.

"How did you end up in Whiskey Springs?" he asked.
I slowly opened my eyes and looked over at him.
"I don't think I can tell you," I said.

20

GREYSON

*N*oelle's little apartment over the ice cream shop was small. Small, but spacious and tidy.

The furniture was old—last century old—and threadbare in places, but the apartment had a clean, pine scent.

There was a fireplace, but it didn't look it had ever been used.

The view from the large uncovered windows was spectacular. Even from here on the sofa, I could see the glow of the moon as it settled over the mountain peaks in the distance.

She surprised me when she sat down. She surprised me even more with her answer.

It was a simple question. I merely asked how she ended up in Whiskey Springs.

"I don't think I can tell you."

It sounded mysterious and like maybe there was a caper involved.

"Why not?" I asked, keeping my tone purposely light. "Is it a secret?"

She smiled and opened her eyes just enough to look at me.

"I suppose it is." But she closed her eyes and didn't say

anything else to clarify.

The wind howled outside, as it tended to do up in this high elevation. I could hope that it meant there was a snow storm on the way, but I knew it did not. The weather forecasters would know if it was going to snow and they didn't have anything to say about it. Since weather forecasters lived for snow and bad weather, it was most definitely not going to snow tonight.

Noelle looked so vulnerable sitting over there on her side of the sofa. A little bit lost even.

I followed my gut. Didn't question my impulse. Just scooted over to sit next to her and put my arm around her shoulders in a companionable—comfortable—fashion. I shouldn't have done it. She could ask me to leave. To say I had stepped over her boundaries. But we had claimed to be companions. And this was companionable.

But with her eyes still closed, she leaned her head against my shoulder. It was such a smooth, natural movement. We sat together like a couple that had been together for ages.

I sighed.

Her head fit perfectly against my shoulder.

This wasn't getting better. It was getting worse.

Getting close to her was not in the best interest of either of us.

"I ended up here by accident," she said, so softly I barely heard her words.

I looked down, trying to see her face. Her eyes were still closed and she looked serene, despite her words that sounded a bit ominous to me.

"What do you mean by accident?"

"I am not supposed to talk about it."

My mind raced with possibilities. Maybe she was witness protection. Maybe she was being stalked. Maybe she'd lost her memory.

"You can't just say that and then leave me hanging like this."

I felt her smile against me. Just a little.

"So… you took a wrong turn at Albuquerque?" I asked, trying to lighten the mood.

She straightened and looked at me, her brows furrowed. "What—?"

"Nothing," I said. "It's just a saying my brothers and I have."

I straightened, too, and faced her, taking both her hands in mine.

"Are you in danger?" I asked. "Are you in some kind of trouble? Because if you are, I can help you."

She nodded. Then seemed to change her mind and shook her head.

"Not danger," she said, then added with a little smile. "Trouble, probably yes."

I looked toward the door leading to downstairs. I felt compelled to go back downstairs. Check the locks. But she was holding on to my hands like a lifeline, so I stayed put.

"What can I do?" I asked, looking into her eyes. Looking for answers to questions I didn't understand.

"Nothing." She pulled her eyes from mine and looked away. "For the moment, at least, I think I am safe."

"I don't exactly feel comforted by that."

She did smile then and some of the tension seemed to drain from the room.

"No one knows I am here."

"What about your family?"

She shook her head, harder this time. "No. They are the ones who can't know."

"You're hiding from your family?" I didn't feel like I was getting anywhere with her. Nowhere at all.

But then she met my gaze again and I saw the pain there. "Yes."

21

NOELLE

Dear Nicholas,

Everything is different now. My world has flipped upside down. But please listen to me. I made the right choice. Do not let Father tell you who to marry. That is the worst thing you can do. It leads to unbearable loneliness.

— Noelle, written to her younger brother the day after she fell in love

The overhead light was on, but I knew the mountains were out there. Standing tall and regal with their crowns of snow. Somehow I found comfort when I looked out at them. Perhaps they reminded me of home. Of the home that I carried in my heart with warm memories. Not the home that haunted me now, keeping me away.

Sitting here on the old, but comfortable, sofa next to Greyson, I felt safe. As long he had his arm around me, I felt free to let the rest of the world fade away into the background.

It was as though it couldn't touch me here. As long as I was with Greyson.

I wanted to tell him everything, but I couldn't. I had been too well trained to say nothing. So much so that the words would not cross my lips. They couldn't.

He wanted to help me, but he couldn't help me with the one thing that I struggled with.

My father.

My legacy.

My heritage.

I shivered.

"Can I make you something warm to drink?"

I nodded. "There's tea in the cupboard."

He left me sitting there and went into my kitchen like he was in his own home.

I watched him add water to the teakettle and place it on a gas burner.

The sounds, the actions, were comforting. He found two mugs and set them out.

Then he came back to the sofa and looked down at me.

He took the blanket I had brought in for him, shook it out, and wrapped it around my shoulders.

"Thank you," I said, looking up at him.

Then he knelt in front of me, looking into my eyes. "Let me help you."

I shook my head.

"I can. I have the resources."

"I am okay. I just have to stay here. To stay out of sight."

"For how long?" He took my hands in his. "How long do you have to stay hidden like this?"

"I don't know." I did know, sort of, but I didn't want to tell him.

"I understand you don't want to lose your job," he said. "But you don't have to worry about that."

I looked in his eyes, trying to figure out what he meant. Then it occurred to me. That part I could tell him.

"It's not just a job. I own Smedley's Ice Cream Shop."

I saw the surprise in his expression. Felt it in the way he held my hands—his hold loosened. Maybe telling him had not been the best idea.

"How?"

I took a deep breath and let the words spill out. "It started out as a job. Mrs. Whitman hired me about ten months ago. I did not know it, but she was thinking about retiring. About moving to Florida. Then I made the hot chocolate ice cream for her. She made me manager. Then before I knew what was happening, she up and moved to Florida. It was not long before the deed arrived." I took a breath and looked into his eyes. "The deed to the shop."

"She gave it to you?"

"She said she had gotten what she needed out of it. That she no longer wanted it hanging over her head. That I should take it and make something of my life."

Those particular words still stung a bit. Mrs. Whitman didn't know much about me. Just like everyone else, she just made her own assumptions. And I let her. I had no choice.

"So…" Greyson was watching me carefully. "You didn't want the ice cream shop?"

"I like it okay. It's just…" I looked at him carefully. I trusted this man. Maybe too much, but I trusted him.

"I don't need it."

22

GREYSON

The tea kettle went off, shattering the peacefulness that surrounded us.

I got to my feet and quickly removed it from the heat.

Making the tea gave me a few minutes to think.

It was, however, going to take more than a few minutes of thinking to figure this out.

I was so lost.

Noelle was somehow in trouble with her family. Hiding. And as a result, she had ended up here. The old owner had taken a liking to her and had given her the ice cream shop. A generous offer, but I had heard of such things. The old woman probably had no heirs and as Noelle said, she had no use for it. It had served its purpose for her.

I poured hot water into the two mugs. Added some honey. I probably should have asked how she took her tea, but I figured if the girl had a honey bear in her kitchen, she probably took honey in her tea.

I took my time stirring each one. Trying to come up with something appropriate to say.

My phone, still in my pocket, chimed. It wasn't Tiffany. I could tell by the tone. So I pulled it out and looked at it.

It was from Mr. Williams. He apologized for not getting in touch with me already. But if I needed a place to spend the night, I was welcome in his home.

I looked over my shoulder at Noelle sitting on the sofa, huddled beneath the blanket.

She looked up and smiled a little.

There was no way I was leaving her here by herself. She had confided in me and now her problems were mine—whether she liked it or not.

ME: *I think I'm good, but thank you for the offer.*

Then I tucked my phone away, marveling at the irony of it all. I'd spent all day, both Noelle and I both had, trying to find me a room for the night. And now that I was here in her apartment—against my own personal rules—my client had come through with a room.

Such was the way of life.

Still not having a clue what to do about her or even what to say to her, I took the mugs back over to the sofa and after handing one to her, sat down beside her.

She wrapped her fingers around the warm mug and held it up to her face for the warmth.

So beautiful. And she had no idea just how beautiful she was.

I wanted to take her away from here. To protect her from the world. To keep her safe.

My mother would say I was being fanciful.

And I was. But I didn't care.

Noelle didn't want to tell me everything. Not yet. Anyway.

I would give her time.

I had found her for a reason. Mr. Williams had delayed his flight. And I had stopped in at the ice cream shop.

Everything happened for a reason.

My grandfather, Noah Worthington, taught me that. *Never turn your back on fate, he'd say. If I'd turned my back on fate, I never would have found your grandmother. Nothing happens by accident.*

I'd had that so drilled into my brain from a very young age, that when I looked at Noelle, all I saw was fate.

She sipped her tea and looked up at me.

"Do you need to go?" she asked.

Reaching out, I tucked a lock of hair behind her ear. She closed her eyes and her lips parted.

"I'm not leaving you," I said.

She blinked, opening her emerald green eyes and locking them onto mine.

I was lost.

"Thank you," she whispered.

I sat, holding my own mug in my hands. It was only then that I realized that Noelle didn't have a television, but there was a notebook computer sitting on the desk.

"What am I going to do with you?" I asked.

23

NOELLE

*T*he mug Greyson handed me was one I had gotten from Starbuck's when I first moved here, but I'd used it so much the images had faded off and now it just looked like an old white mug.

I wrapped my fingers around the warm mug and soaked in the warmth. It wasn't the heat from the mug that warmed me so much as it was knowing that Greyson had made the tea for me.

I hadn't even sipped it yet, but I knew it was perfect. It smelled like peppermint. My favorite tea anytime of the year.

"What am I going to do with you?" he asked the words, but he wasn't talking to me. He was staring into his mug of tea and he said it so softly I almost thought I imagined it.

But I spent too much time alone to not pay attention to others.

I liked having him here, but it was still a disruption.

With him here, I saw everything differently—through his eyes.

I saw old-fashioned furniture covered in snags that needed to be updated.

He made the cozy apartment seem smaller than it normally seemed.

Greyson was so full of life. Larger than life.

I almost smiled. I had just been wondering what I was going to do with *him*.

I needed to go to my bedroom for the night. To leave him here.

He would take care of himself. I was certain of that.

But he was like a magnet pulling me to him. I didn't want to be apart from him.

Maybe it was because I had been so alone for so long. Only having customers to talk to, especially now that Mrs. Whitman had moved away to Florida. That and my monthly letters to my younger brother. I wasn't sure that counted as talking to someone since I never heard back.

Still. He and I were close. I missed him more now at Christmas than I had any other time.

But as long as I was here, he was safe. I was doing the right thing by being here.

"I should get some sleep," I said.

He didn't answer me, so I decided that I should at least pretend to drink my tea.

I took a sip. It was a simple peppermint tea, but it was perfect.

Just like the day. The day had been perfect.

How was it that just one day could upset a girl's life so completely?

When I looked at him, my heart swelled and drunken butterflies fluttered in my stomach.

I had never felt like this before. I was twenty-five, but I had been sheltered. Home schooled. Tutored in everything considered important. Piano. Literature. Formal dance.

I knew how to hold a conversation with anyone at a dinner party. I had brought those skills with me to the ice cream shop.

I knew how to make small talk. How to ask people about things that interested them.

But more than just small talk, with a stranger, I wasn't so sure. Once we got past the usual small talk, I had to figure it out for myself.

I hadn't had trouble talking to Greyson all day. But now that we were alone, I was at a loss for words. He wanted to know things about me. Why I was here.

But those were things I couldn't tell him just yet.

Maybe one day.

Beyond that, I wasn't schooled in intimate conversations with men.

There had never been a reason to.

There had never been a reason for me to go on dates and meet eligible men.

There was a reason because I had been betrothed since birth.

24

GREYSON

*N*oelle and I sat quietly sipping our tea. I felt there were so many things unsaid.

And yet, oddly enough, there were so many things I didn't feel we had to say.

If we were in Houston and this was ordinary date, I would have kissed her already.

But this wasn't Houston and this wasn't a date at all, at least not officially.

As my tea began to grow cold, I took it to the sink. I didn't see a dishwasher, so I washed it, dried it, and put it up.

My mother had always taught me to put things back the way I had found them.

I was stalling. I was stalling and I knew it.

I was giving myself time to think. But it wasn't working. My brain wasn't working. It was on some kind of hiatus.

Taking a break. Just being around Noelle did that to me.

I had to get her to her room before I bent my own rules and kissed her.

It would be wrong to kiss a girl I was probably never going

to see again. Thinking about it that way helped me with my resolve. I had to be strong.

The little voice in the back of my head was not helping. *You're a pilot. With Skye Travels. You can fly anyplace you want to anytime.*

The little voice was wrong, of course. I was a pilot and I did work for Skye Travels. And yes, my family did own Skye Travels. But I did not own my own airplane. I didn't want to. I never ruled out future possibilities, but at the moment I had no need to.

I was doing what I wanted to do. Fly. And I was fortunate enough to have flights five to seven days a week. I liked being in the air. I didn't need the headaches, like airplane ownership, that went along with it. As a result, I flew where I was assigned.

It suited me, I told myself again.

It had never bothered me that I couldn't just hop in a plane an airplane and fly wherever I wanted. My aunts and uncles did that sometimes. Cousins, too.

I'd had no need.

Maybe I had a need now.

But I couldn't just do that. I had responsibilities.

Arguing with myself was counterproductive to say the least. I took a deep breath and pulled myself together.

Noelle was watching me, but pretending not to.

"Can I walk you to your bedroom?" I asked, standing in front of her and holding out a hand.

"Of course," she said, placing a hand in mine.

I tried to ignored the feel of her hand in mine. Tried not to think about how natural it felt.

I led her to her bedroom door… it was only a few feet… and stopped.

"Goodnight, my fair one," I said, pressing my lips lightly on her forehead. Her skin beneath my lips was smooth and soft.

And she smelled like gardenias along with a faint scent of vanilla and... cocoa.

"Goodnight," she said, her voice soft.

Then she pushed away from me, went into her bedroom, and closed the door. I didn't move. I just stood there. Frozen.

Kissing her once on the forehead did not count.

It did not count as a kiss.

I stood there, needing to hear her moving around in her room.

It made no sense, but I needed to wait. Maybe it was because she had told me she could be in trouble.

I should have checked the room before she closed herself inside.

Then I heard water running in what had to be her bathroom sink.

Slowly letting out a breath I didn't know I was holding, I went back to the sofa, sat down, and pulled out my phone.

It was an hour later in Houston, but I knew exactly who could help me. There were two people actually. My grandfather Noah Worthington and my Uncle Quinn.

Since it was late, I went with Uncle Quinn. He was most likely to still be awake and available.

I quickly composed a text message.

ME: *I know it's late, but I need your help with something.*

25

NOELLE

*A*fter closing the door between myself and Greyson, I stood there, leaning against the cool wood, my hand still on the doorknob until my heart rate slowed down to a steady rate.

I quietly turned the lock. I didn't feel like I needed to lock the door. I just felt like I *should* lock the door.

I couldn't stand here all night. I needed to pull myself together and get into bed.

But first I went into the bathroom and splashed cold water on my face.

The cold water cleared my senses and helped me collect my thoughts.

Greyson had kissed me goodnight on the forehead.

A kiss on the forehead didn't really count as a kiss. I could, however, have tilted my head up just so and his lips would have touched mine.

But that would have made a mess of things. It would have made it even more difficult for me after he left tomorrow.

I would never see him again.

I had to accept that.

It was really quite simple.

He lived on the other side of the country and I... I wasn't sure what the future held for me. My future was too uncertain for me to bring anyone into my life in any capacity.

Even if I did decide to bring someone into my life, it should be someone other than Greyson. He deserved better. He deserved someone without a history like mine. Without the expectations that my life brought with it.

It didn't lessen the sting.

My father had done me a grave disservice by not allowing me to date like normal people.

Or maybe he hadn't.

Perhaps because I was betrothed at birth I had been indoctrinated into the belief that there was someone for everyone.

I hadn't needed to date.

Even now I didn't feel like I needed to date.

Even if I wasn't betrothed to someone, now that I had met Greyson, I believed even more strongly that there was one person for everyone.

If I wasn't betrothed to someone. If I lived in Houston. If my family was normal.

If. If. If.

Perhaps even in another world. In another time. Greyson and I could be together.

But not in this world. Not in this time.

It wasn't possible.

I had to let him go.

And even though I had to let him go, I would cherish this perfect day for the rest of my life.

I could hold it close to my heart. Replaying it over and over.

I could still feel his lips against my forehead. So soft. So firm.

I sat in the reading chair in front of my window and stared

out at the mountain range in the distance. Snow clouds were gathering around the peaks, hinting of the possibility of snow tonight.

According to the weather forecasters, the snow would be confined to the high country for the next few days. They typically got it right. Amazingly so.

It would have been nice to have a white Christmas. But maybe it was better that it wasn't. A white Christmas would be bittersweet for me. It would be beautiful, but it would make me miss home even harder.

I leaned my elbows on the window ledge and rested my chin on my hands.

There would be no sleep for me tonight.

My perspective was off-kilter. I'd taken a job at a random ice cream shop. Became the manager. Then became the owner.

And none of that affected me the way a simple kiss on the forehead had.

I needed to think.

There would be no sleeping for me tonight.

Not with Greyson Fleming on the other side of my bedroom door.

26

GREYSON

I lay awake, staring out at the full moon over the tall rugged mountain peaks, holding my phone in my hands.

I didn't hear from Uncle Quinn, so he must have already gone to bed.

He would get back with me in the morning.

Either way, I knew what I had to do.

Noelle was quiet on the other side of the bedroom door.

I had gone back downstairs. Checked all the locks. Even checked the window locks.

Curiosity about her burned inside me.

I tapped my phone and wondered if I should leave it alone.

It was really none of my business who Noelle really was. None of my business what kind of trouble she might be in with her family.

It wasn't my place to daydream about kissing her.

Just that simple kiss on her forehead had almost been too much. It would have been so easy to shift just a little, merely a few inches, and my lips could have been on hers.

It would have been so easy. Too easy.

But it would not have been right.

Not for either one of us.

Noelle was a lady. And a lady deserved more than a kiss from a random stranger.

And as much as I didn't want it to be so, a random stranger was exactly what I was.

Just as I was thinking about falling asleep, another text came in from Tiffany. I opened the text with a groan.

TIFFANY: *I know you aren't answering me. And that's okay. I understand. But...*

There was something different about this message. Something about it that I felt I shouldn't ignore.

I stared at the thought bubbles, unable to look away. The message—if a message could *sound* serious—sounded more serious than the messages she had been sending me all day. Those had been pouty messages about her dress and how the party was going—without me—but this one was different.

The thought bubbles vanished. I started to compose a reply, but then her message come through.

TIFFANY: *Things have been kinda crazy. And I think that everyone assumes that you and I are staying in touch so that I would be the one to tell you.*

What? Tell me what? I sat up. My heart pounded dangerously against my chest. Something was wrong. I could sense it all the way down to my toes.

But all I could do was to wait. I almost just called her

TIFFANY: *Grandpa Noah collapsed during the party. They rushed him to the hospital. I'm sorry, but that's all I know. I'm not family, so they aren't letting me in the waiting room at the hospital.*

My fingers trembled as I picked up the water bottle on the floor beside me. The sip of water didn't wash away the metallic taste in my mouth.

Grandpa Noah. Hospital. Collapsed.

I tossed off the blanket and stood up. Paced to the window, to the door, and back to the sofa.

ME: *You don't know anything?*

TIFFANY: *All I know if that there must a hundred people here at the hospital.*

I tossed the phone down as though it had burned me. Paced the room again.

My brain was going into automatic.

I needed to get home.

I folded the blanket. Put on my boots.

Sat down again and pulled my iPad out of my bag.

Houston. I needed to get to Houston.

I had a Phenom at my disposal a few miles away at the Whiskey Springs airport.

My fingers still trembling, I filed a flight plan. A night flight.

Mr. Williams was nothing more than a brief thought in the back of my mind.

At this point, he wasn't my concern.

Everything gathered up, shrugging into my jacket, my woolen coat over it, I stared at Noelle's door for a full five seconds.

It was almost Midnight.

There was no need for me to wake her only to tell her that I was leaving. Immediately.

There was one problem though. I couldn't lock up the shop from the outside. Not without a key. I couldn't—wouldn't—leave the door downstairs unlocked. Not even with her bedroom door locked. Too much could go wrong.

I paced to the desk. It stood in front of a glass door that led to a back stairway. The lock was functionable from the inside.

That was the answer. I slid the desk out just enough to slip past to the door.

As I slid out the door, locking it behind me, several thoughts occurred to me.

I didn't have Noelle's phone number... I could have written her a note...

But the cold air slapping me in the face only increased my urgency. I don't know what I thought I could do, but I needed to be there for Grandpa.

I needed to get home—to the hospital—to be near my grandfather.

With that singular focus, I vanished into the night.

27

NOELLE

I'd fallen asleep in spite of a certainty that I wouldn't be able to.

I woke with a splash of morning sunlight across my face along with that fleeting sense that everything was alright with the world.

That fleeting feeling that never lasted past the barrage of thoughts coming on its heels that reminded me of all the problems I had to deal with that day.

But today, that feeling lasted a bit longer than usual.

I smiled to myself and stretched.

Greyson Fleming was on the other side of that door and he might be flying out today, but that didn't mean we couldn't have a few hours together.

I glanced at the clock. It was already six fifteen. The sooner I got out there, the more time we would have together. My shop opened at ten, but I didn't have much to do to get it ready. Greyson had cleaned everything up last night.

We'd go to breakfast. I certainly didn't have anything here worth eating. Maybe a breakfast bar or a banana at most.

Anticipation running through my veins, I jumped into the shower.

Maybe he would ask for my cell phone number. Maybe a lot of things.

Maybe he would kiss me goodbye with a promise to return soon. Maybe even on the lips.

Sighing, I finished rinsing my hair and turned off the water.

I had more romantic notions tucked inside me than I had known. It was… interesting. And unexpected.

After blow drying my hair, I added a bit of wave with a thermal brush and then put on some red lipstick that I was told flattered my complexion.

I stared at the clothes in my closet before choosing a red flowy skirt that fell below my knees in the front and nearly to the floor in the back and a matching red sweater. I was going to regret wearing a skirt, especially if we went outside, but the outfit was festive and pretty.

And I felt festive and pretty.

More so, at least, since setting foot in Whiskey Springs.

It was the day before Christmas Eve AND I would be seeing Greyson.

I put on some black lace up combat style boots and declared myself ready to face the day.

The first thing I noticed before my fingers even released the doorknob was that my desk was moved.

Someone had slid the desk away from the door that led to the outside stairway entrance that I never used.

A bolt of fear shot through my veins, but I could see from here that the door was locked. Letting go of the door knob, my heart racing with dread, I walked over to the sofa and looked over it.

My worse fear, one I had not even been aware of, had come true. The blanket was neatly folded on one end of the sofa, the pillow stacked on top of it.

And Greyson was not there.

I looked from the sofa to the door.

I walked slowly to the desk, then to the kitchen counter. I made a complete turn around my little apartment. There was no note anywhere. Nothing. Not a word.

Greyson had fled.

I sat down hard on the sofa and simply stared into space, not seeing anything. Not seeing the bright cheerful morning sunlight streaming through my uncovered windows. I saw nothing but emptiness.

Without so much as a word.

He was gone.

28

GREYSON

*B*y the time I was well on my way, flying back toward Houston, the soft shades of dawn were on the horizon. To me it was the most beautiful time of day.

One I admittedly rarely saw unless forced to get up early. But when I did, like now, I was awed by nature's beauty.

Flying east, I flew into the sunrise. In the western movies, the hero and heroine always rode off into the sunset, but there was something magical about flying into the sunrise.

Unfortunately, at the moment, I wasn't in a place to fully appreciate it.

The lump in my throat was painful and remnants of the metallic taste were still there. I hadn't eaten. Hadn't even taken the time to stop for coffee.

I was exhausted. Exhausted but too amped up to stop. I was running on adrenalin.

Not that there was a lot of running involved in actually sitting in the cockpit, but my mind did not seem to know that.

My thoughts raced.

I felt like I was living in a nightmare.

I couldn't help thinking that I should have been there for Grandpa.

Then I would remind myself that there would have been nothing I could have done even if I had been there.

I was in hell.

My thoughts wandered occasionally to Noelle, but every time they went in that direction, they bounced back.

She did not belong in this nightmare.

She was everything good and perfect.

I would think about her later. After I was no longer in this nightmare. So that way there wouldn't be an association between her and this.

Why hadn't my family contacted me? They were probably like me. Unable to think past anything other than the next breath.

When I landed at the airport in Houston and taxied up to the private Skye Travels terminal, it was eerily deserted. On any given day, there were airplanes coming and going. Or at least sitting on the tarmac preparing for departure. But right now the tarmac was empty.

No activity.

I parked the plane, raced through my post-flight checklist and took off at a sprint to my car waiting in the private parking lot.

As I closed the car door, I realized that I didn't know where to go. Which hospital?

I sent a quick text to Tiffany.

ME: *Where?*

She responded quickly.

And I was off.

I didn't read any other texts and I didn't call anyone. I couldn't.

If the news was bad, I did not want to know it.

I had the thought, probably irrational as it was, that if I could just get to him everything would be okay.

It was still early enough that I was ahead of the morning rush hour.

I made it to the hospital in record time.

As I parked my car in the hospital parking lot, I recognized several cars. Aunts. Uncles. Cousins.

I briefly took comfort in that. They were still here. Then my thoughts scrambled and I couldn't make sense of whether that was a good thing or not.

But I was here. I jumped out of my car and sprinted to the door.

As I reached the hospital doors, it belatedly occurred to me that it would have been nice to have Noelle here with me.

I shook off the thought.

I would think about her later.

29

NOELLE

Christmas Eve

hristmas had always been my favorite time of the year. The festive music that tugged at the heart, bringing back memories of happy holidays of childhood. The twinkling lights draped across everything that moved. The sparkle of magic that shimmered in the air.

Until now. Right now the very things that had always brought me joy were bringing tears to my eyes.

I was downstairs in the ice cream shop, standing behind the cold marble counter, leaning across it with my elbows on it. Not at all ladylike. But one thing I had learned living in the small town of Whiskey Springs. No one cared.

I'd just opened the shop less than half an hour ago and already there were six people in the shop. A family and some young people.

The one man I had fallen in love with had vanished in the night. So, it seemed, at least to me at the moment, that

I had very little to lose. The worst thing that could happen... my father would drag me back to the island and force me to marry the son of the man who owned a nearby island.

At this particular moment, I'd like to see him try it.

I was a business owner. Part of the community of Whiskey Springs. I was making money of my own through the ice cream shop.

And I had experienced true love. I felt different. Like somehow I understood now what all the fairy tales were about. Although my heart ached, I felt stronger. A strength, perhaps, that came with apathy.

The bell over the door jingled, sending me standing upright. Others may not care that I had poor posture, but I was too well-bred to not care for myself.

A young mother ordered two small vanilla chocolate swirl ice creams. One for herself and one for the son standing at her knee.

As she swiped her credit card and I waited for payment to process, my gaze strayed to the window.

I blinked. Then froze. Then blinked again.

"No," I murmured to myself.

"No?" the young mother asked, looking alarmed. "Is something wrong?"

"No," I said, forcing a smile and sparing her a quick glance. "Everything is fine. Please. Enjoy your ice cream."

Watching me warily, she thanked me and led her son to a table as far away from the counter as she could get.

I didn't move. I was transfixed where I stood.

I fully expected the young man standing outside my window to vanish at any moment. To simply keep walking like so many curious tourists did.

As I stood there, hardly daring to blink, one song blended into another and yet the man still did not move.

I walked around the counter and stood in the middle of my shop.

If the customers watched me with perplexed expressions, I didn't notice.

I didn't care.

Then the young man smiled and moved swiftly to the door.

I watched him, recognizing everything. The way he looked. The way he moved. But he was taller. Maybe a little more filled out. A year made a lot of difference in a fifteen—no sixteen—year old boy.

Nicholas wrapped his arms me and hugged me so hard he picked me up.

My most salient thought was how had my little brother grown so much in just one year.

But instead, when my feet hit the ground, I asked. "What are you doing here?"

30

GREYSON

I sat at one of the tables at the Sky House Restaurant and Bar—no relation to Skye Travels—with my oldest brother Daniel and my younger sister Isabella.

It was mid-morning and the place was filled with the breakfast crowd—overall subdued, but still with a magical undercurrent that only existed at Christmas.

There would be a lot of people traveling today. Coming and going to be with family. But today none of us—all three of us pilots—would be flying.

We did something we rarely did. We ordered mimosas all around. But at the moment, none of us cared enough to worry about it.

For one thing it was Christmas Eve morning. And that wasn't even the good news.

None of us said anything as we waited for our drinks to arrive.

We were, as a group, just too exhausted.

After the mimosas arrived, we all took a sip.

But I pushed mine away. I was sitting too close to the

airport. Even though I wasn't flying today, I knew there was a possibility. There was always a possibility.

My sister, Isabella did the same. She didn't drink anyway.

Daniel held up a hand to get the server's attention.

"Can we get a round of just regular orange juice?" he asked, then continued to sip his own drink.

As Isabella and I watched him, he just shrugged.

"You weren't there," he said.

He had that right. We all had our own experiences. I had been in Whiskey Springs. Isabella had been flying.

But Daniel had been at the fundraiser where Grandpa had collapsed.

"What happened?" I asked, looking at Daniel. "What really happened?"

Daniel ran a hand through his hair and blew out a breath. "Exhaustion. That's what the doctors think. But they're going to be running a whole bunch of tests."

"I should hope so," I said. I'd heard the same thing. More tests. I also knew that sometimes tests didn't provide all the answers.

"They definitely need to run some tests on his heart," Isabella said.

Daniel and I both just looked blankly at her.

"What?" she said. "He's no spring chicken. It could easily be his heart. Especially since they said it's exhaustion."

Daniel and I looked at each other. Isabella sat back and crossed her arms, glaring at us. "I know we all have the same brother named Jack."

Our brother, Jack, was Dr. Jack Fleming. Studying to be a psychiatrist, but a physician nonetheless. He'd actually spent a year doing a fellowship in Whiskey Springs.

Daniel laughed as he took another sip of his mimosa. "I'm surprised you actually listen to him."

"I'm glad at least one of us does," I said.

"What's that supposed to mean?" Daniel asked.

"It means just that. The more we can learn from each other, the better off we'll be."

"Well, I guess the three of us pilots can't learn much from each other," Daniel said. "Hard to learn from a doctor or a venture capitalist who aren't living in the same town."

"I think we can still learn from each other," Isabella said.

"Agreed," I said.

"What is this? Pick on Daniel day?"

Isabella and I just looked at our brother. To make a fair assessment, he looked like hell.

"I guess we should leave him alone," I said. "He's had a rather hard time of it."

"I have," Daniel said. "I'm just glad Jenna was here."

"Yeah," I sat back, suddenly thinking about Noelle. "Damn," I muttered to myself.

I looked around at the people in the restaurant. So many people on their way to see their loved ones. Families traveling together.

And I had left the one I had fallen in love with behind. I'd had no choice.

"Is there something you want to tell us?" Isabella asked.

"Nuh-uh," I said quickly, shaking my head.

Daniel was giving me one of his looks. Then he looked over at Isabella. "He's lying," he said. "There's something he's not telling us."

The server brought our orange juice.

Isabella yawned, covering her mouth with her hand.

"You should get some rest," I said.

"I will," she said, yawning again. "We have time for a nap before meeting at Grandpa's tonight."

"I'm not sure he needs all that much excitement," I said.

"Well, I'll be there. Can't leave him alone at Christmas."

"He'll hardly be alone," I said.

"I'm just glad Jenna is here with me."

Their two statements melded together in my head. And once again, I thought about Noelle. Alone in Whiskey Springs.

It was wrong.

I looked from one sibling to the other. Tapped my fingers on the table.

Daniel had Jenna. In fact, out of the five of us, Isabella and I were the only two who didn't have anyone.

But I have someone.

The thought came unexpected and unbidden.

"Are you alright?" Isabella asked, looking at me with concern.

I sat up straight. "There's actually something I have to do."

"Right now?" Daniel asked. "I thought you were tired."

When I pulled out my iPad, both of my siblings watched me with alarm.

"Where are you going?" Isabella asked.

Daniel sat back. "He's not going anywhere. It's Christmas." But he sounded uncertain.

I ignored both of them.

There were some things a man just had to do for himself.

31

NOELLE

*N*icholas turned out to be good help in the ice cream shop. Unexpectedly so.

We talked a little as we worked. The shop was busy. Voices and laughter mingled with the Christmas music to create a festive background.

"What are you doing here?" I asked Nicholas.

He grinned. "I found you."

I shook my head. "But how?"

He lowered his voice. "I can't tell you. Maybe later."

The morning drifted into afternoon with similar conversations. Still. I got nothing out of him. He would tell me later. When we weren't so busy.

Whatever it was, he didn't seem particularly disturbed by it so I didn't think he was in any kind of trouble. But I really wanted to know how he had found me. If he had found me, then it was possible my father could find me.

But by mid-afternoon, I could tell that Nicholas was getting restless.

There was a lot of repetition involved in this business. Take orders. Fill them. Clean up the tables. I found it comforting, but Nicholas, obviously not so much. At least not right now.

"Maybe you should take a walk around town," I suggested after I handed a customer an ice cream hot chocolate. One thing only I knew how to make.

"I'm good," he said.

"No, really. It's Christmas Eve. You should walk around. Check things out."

"Are you sure?" He wiped his hands on a cloth. "I hate to leave you alone with all this."

All this was down to only half a dozen customers. A breeze.

I looked at him sideways. "You do know that I do this every day? Right?"

"I find it a little hard to believe," he said, with an impish shrug.

"Seriously?"

"You were always studying or reading something."

I stopped in my task of refilling the napkin dispenser and looked at him with a hand resting on one hip. "I guess that is true," I admitted.

A group of teenage girls walked by outside, laughing and obviously having a good time.

"Maybe I will take that turn about town." He met my gaze.

"Good," I said, trying to ignore the fact that my little brother was obviously interested in checking out the girls who just walked past.

I waved a hand at him. "Go on. Get out of here."

Grinning, he grabbed his coat and did just that.

"If I don't see you before, I'll meet you at the Christmas Eve party at the high school gym."

"After that," he said. "Maybe I'll answer your question."

"Boys," I muttered under my breath. But I sighed in relief. Not so much that my brother was gone, but that I could stop pretending to be happy. Stop pretending that everything was okay.

I leaned on the counter and, after a quick scan to check the status of the customers—to make sure no one needed anything and no one looked suspicious, I allowed myself to sigh.

It was so hard pretending that my heart wasn't broken. I didn't want to say anything to my brother. He was too young to understand.

Greyson had left without even so much as getting my cell phone number.

He knows how to call Smedley's Ice Cream Shop.

I stared at the offending land line. A quick Google search would give him the phone number here. He could reach me if he wanted to.

I glanced at the clock. It was almost time for me to close up anyway. Everything in town closed early on Christmas Eve. People were either making their way to the Christmas Eve party or they were home with family.

Walking over to the door, I turned the sign to closed. I couldn't help looking both ways up and down the sidewalk. Even across the street. Looking for... something. Looking for Greyson.

Since I'd been in Whiskey Springs, I had a habit of scanning for suspicious people who might recognize me, but in the past two days, I had begun to scan instead—maybe in addition to —Greyson.

I didn't understand why he had left my apartment in the night. And if he was still in town, then he obviously did not want to see me.

Maybe he had decided he didn't want to get so close to me.

There were so many possibilities. But no matter what the truth was, I knew I had to leave it alone. I had to let him go just as he had let me go.

After the last customer left, I turned the lock.

It felt so final.

It meant that Greyson was not coming back.

So much for the magic of Christmas Eve. There was no magic in the air tonight. Not for me.

This was the worst Christmas Eve ever. If not for my brother being here, well... I didn't want to think about it.

I cleaned up what needed to be done, then went upstairs to get dressed for the party. I'd wavered on whether or not I wanted to go, but I knew I needed to go. For myself.

Since I had changed into blue jeans yesterday after I discovered Greyson gone, tonight I would wear my red high-low skirt. I even put on the sparkly diamond stud earrings that I never wore. I was always afraid that someone would question how I was able to buy such nice things. Not to my face, of course, but people would talk and I was trying my best to avoid drawing attention to myself.

Tonight I was determined to feel like a princess.

I suppose I was feeling bold. Or maybe I just didn't care so much right now.

Two days ago the world had been so full of promise... the day had been perfect and now things seemed hopeless.

I sprayed some perfume in the air and walked through it.

It did not matter, I told myself.

At least now I knew what to look for. I knew what falling in love felt like.

If I let myself be open to it, it could happen again. Yet the little pep talk I gave myself did nothing to help my broken heart.

No matter how I knew I needed to forget about Greyson and move on, I knew that it would never happen. When it was time, I would find someone to be content with. But I had found my soulmate... my one great love... and I would be content. Somehow. I would be content.

I walked out of my bedroom into my little living room and shrieked.

There was someone at the glass door behind my desk.

And that someone was Greyson Fleming.

32

GREYSON

*T*he cold mountain wind whipped around me. It wasn't snowing. Yet. But even I, a Houstonian, could feel snow in the air. The air was moist and left a fine layer of mist over my coat that seemed to be freezing.

As far as Christmas Eves went, this was most definitely a frosty one.

I stood at the top of the stairway at the back door to Noelle's apartment. It was locked, of course, as it should be. She had slid the desk back into place, as she should have.

If I touched my tongue to the frosty glass, it would probably stick to it. I must be delirious to think something so crazy.

Either way, I must be insane.

Everything was just as it should have been. Except that I was here.

I was supposed to be at home, specifically at my grandparents' house for their annual Christmas Eve gathering.

But my grandfather was resting, as he should be. If his children and grandchildren would let him. Which was somewhat doubtful.

But while the rest of my family was headed to the

Worthington house for Christmas, I had gotten back in the Phenom and flown straight back to Whiskey Springs.

I probably should have called before just showing up. But I had felt compelled to be here. Just compelled. It was the only way I could explain it.

The front door to the ice cream shop was closed, so I had retraced my steps to the back door. It was the way I had left, anyway, so it seemed like the most appropriate way to return.

But I didn't see Noelle anywhere. I must have missed her.

As I still debated what I should do, I saw her.

Noelle swept out of her bedroom, wearing a red dress. Her hair framing the face that had become dear to me in such a short time.

When she saw me standing there, she froze. And I knew I had startled her. That had not been my intent. The fact that it should have occurred to me, but didn't should have told me something.

She was beautiful. Like a princess. Neither one of us moved, but our eyes locked.

I could not help but think that I had made a mistake. I had left without an explanation and there was no way she could understand.

I didn't know whether or not she was close to her family, but since she was here and they were not, I could only think that she was not. And as such, she might not understand the urgency that had driven me two night ago.

It was in some ways a similar urgency to the one that had brought me back to her.

Normally an easygoing guy, I seemed to be suddenly filled with urgencies.

We must have stood there for several seconds. The wind whipped at my scarf and I thought I might be going to freeze standing right here.

Forcing myself to move, I put a palm on her door.

That seemed to spur her into action. She moved quickly, reaching over the desk to unlock the door.

The desk was heavy. I remembered it well.

She slid it just enough that I could reach inside and slide it the rest of the way. Enough that I could squeeze inside.

Now that I was inside I was shivering.

"I'll take your coat," she said. "Sit."

I shrugged out of the frozen coat and handed it to her. As I sat on the sofa where I had attempted to sleep, she hung up my coat in the hall closet to dry.

Then she faced me, her hands on her hips, a perplexed expression her face.

"What are you doing here?"

She looked like an angry goddess. I couldn't help but smile. I tried to hide it, but Noelle missed nothing.

She lifted a brow, waiting for an answer.

33

NOELLE

*M*y heart pounded dangerously in my chest. I put my hands on my hips to keep them steady.

"What are you doing here?" I asked. It seemed to be the question of the day.

After Greyson had vanished in the night, I had not expected to see him again. A man who stole away in the night without a word was not likely to return.

He sat on my sofa as I had instructed. Waiting. Watching me with a little smile that I did not quite understand.

"I'm sorry," he said. "Something happened and I wasn't thinking."

He truly did look apologetic.

"What happened?" I asked. It wasn't, perhaps, polite to ask such personal questions, but the man was in my apartment and I felt like I had a right to know. And besides, he had broken my heart. Surely I needed to at least give him the opportunity to explain himself.

"My grandfather collapsed and was taken to the hospital."

"Oh." All the strength drained from my limbs and I sat down hard next to him. I had a flashback to the day my own grandfather had collapsed and was rushed to the hospital. It was indelibly etched into my memory. One I would have preferred to not have to remember.

"I am so sorry. Is he okay?" I asked, shoving the memory away, my throat dry nonetheless.

"He is home. Recovering," Greyson said. "But I didn't know how serious it might be. All I knew was that I had to get to him. And you… you were asleep." He shrugged.

"So you went to Houston?" The thought that he could have flown to Houston and back in the span of less than thirty-six hours, give or take, astounded me. It shouldn't have. I had grown up on an island and yet I had been so sheltered that a quick flight out and back like that had never been an option, at least not for me.

"Yes." He placed a hand over mine. "I had to go."

I nodded and looked away. "I understand."

We sat in silence for a few more minutes, my thoughts scrambling to find footing. I turned back to him. Looked into his sparkling blue eyes. "Why are you here? Shouldn't you be with your family?"

"Shouldn't you?" he asked, answering a question with a question.

"Probably," I said, turning my hand over so our palms touched. "Actually…"

I blinked and looked away. How did I tell Greyson that I had run away from home and my brother had found me? Perhaps running away from home wasn't quite the best way to put it.

Greyson sat waiting, watching me with enviable patience. He squeezed my hand.

"You can tell me anything," he said. "I won't judge."

I nodded and spoke so softly he may or may not have heard me. "I know."

"Are you in danger?"

I looked back into his eyes. Shook my head. "No." But the single word didn't contain the conviction I planned for it to have. He had asked me that question or a variation of it before. And the answer was the same.

"But there is something troubling you," he said, searching for answers in my eyes.

His gaze was so intense, I wondered if he could see into my very soul.

"You are very astute."

"We have a host of psychologists in the family. It's hard not to pick up things."

I took a deep breath. Decided that I needed to tell him. I didn't want to tell him. It was my secret and I held it well. But now that my brother was here, it was bound to come out anyway.

"I have a secret," I said.

34

GREYSON

The conversation I had had with my siblings that morning came to mind as I watched Noelle. Isabella had been right. A person did pick up things being around family. It was just we all picked up different things.

I picked up an awareness of other people's feelings. I had that awareness sometimes. Not all the time, I had to admit.

But I had it right now.

I could see that Noelle was troubled. I could see it in the way her brow furrowed and the way her gaze darted away from mine.

"A secret?" I asked, purposely smiling to keep my tone light.

Even though her lips curved a little, I couldn't help but worry that her secret was something serious.

It could be anything. She could be hiding from an abusive boyfriend. God help us all if that were the case. I wasn't much of a scrapper, but I could hold my own. And I would protect Noelle with everything I had if it came to that. Hoping against hope that it wasn't that, I tried to think of other things.

A stalker. That wasn't much better. My cousin's girlfriend

had been stalked. It had not been pretty. That was nudging right up there next to the abusive boyfriend thing.

I couldn't even let myself think about the possibility of her having a husband. My brain put a wall blocking that chain of thought, not letting me even go there.

She could be in witness protection, worried about being found.

Her hair color looked natural. If she was in witness protection, surely she would have at least changed the color of her hair. But maybe that was just in the movies. Besides, Whiskey Springs was so small that it would be next to impossible for anyone to find her here unless she had some kind of tie to it. It didn't sound like she did.

I, on the other hand, could never hide out here. I had too many ties.

For one, my grandfather was a major—the major—investor in the airport here. He even housed an airplane here. The Phenom that I was currently flying around in. I hadn't heard from Mr. Williams, so I could only assume that he postponed or canceled his trip.

Three of my siblings had met their true loves here. In Whiskey Springs.

I stopped. Looked over at Noelle.

Whiskey Springs.

Perhaps there was some kind of magic here that brought people together.

Noelle met my gaze and held.

"Did you say you aren't from here?" I asked.

"I don't know if I said or not. But no. I'm not from here."

Neither one of us was from here and yet here we were. Somehow we had found each other here. Not Houston, where I was from, one of the biggest cities in America. Just here. In a most random place. At a random time. No… Not random. At Christmastime.

Just like my three siblings.

I believed in fate and I was developing a healthy respect for the magic of Christmas.

"Are you okay?" she asked. "You look a little pale."

"I'm okay." I turned and took both her hands in mine. "I think you're going to have to tell me your secret. I have an exceptionally inventive mind and I'm coming up with all sorts of things."

"I do not think you could imagine this one if you tried."

"Tell me then," I said.

"I do not know where to start."

"Start at the beginning." I sat back, pretending to look comfortable. Trying to disguise the tension that had me on edge.

The little clock on her wall began to chime the hour.

She looked up, startled. "We can't be late for the Christmas Eve party."

"Seriously?"

"Yes, seriously."

She stood up. If Cinderella was going to the ball, then I was going with her.

I followed her to the coat closet to get my coat. I hated to put it back on, but at least it was dry on the inside. As she grabbed her coat, I caught a glimpse of a long cape lined with fur.

I didn't say anything about it, but it made me wonder. Was this something that had to do with her secret?

Before long, we were heading out, using the main stairway that led down to the shop. We used the back door this time. I didn't even know there was a back door.

There were so many things I didn't know. So many things I had to learn.

But I would learn them. I would learn them because it meant being with Noelle.

35

NOELLE

I had promised Nicholas that I would meet him at the high school gym for the Christmas Eve party. I couldn't leave him on his own. He was so young. Only sixteen.

Like me, he was not from the island. I couldn't expect him to fend for himself.

I wasn't even intentionally stalling. I had been about to tell Greyson my secret when the clock chimed the hour, reminding me that I was supposed to meet my brother.

We stepped out the back door into the icy wind and together, our heads down against the wind, and made our way to the high school gym. The wind had a moisture to it now. It was going to snow. I had no doubt about that.

Modern Christmas music spilled out the gym doors and we heard it long before we reached the doors.

With my hand tucked in the crook of Greyson's elbow, we stepped inside and made our way to the coat check.

Everyone was dressed in their finest outfits. Some of the people there I barely recognized. I was first to admit that I didn't know everyone. Not everyone frequented the ice cream shop and I didn't get out much other than my weekly trip into

Boulder to stock up on supplies and use the library to email Nicholas.

Was that how he had found me? By me using the library? If so, I didn't see how he could have connected the public library in Boulder with me here in Whiskey Springs.

He would tell me.

But first I had to find him.

"Looking for someone?" Greyson asked as I peered through the crowd looking for Nicholas.

"Yes," I said. Then I leaned over and lowered my voice, even though there was no one close enough to hear. "My brother is here."

"Your?" He lowered his voice. "brother? I didn't think you had family here."

"I don't... didn't." I brought my gaze back to his and his handsomeness nearly took my breath away. "Wasn't supposed to. But..." I looked around again, craning my neck. "I really need to find him. He's only sixteen."

Greyson looked around a moment. "Is he as handsome as you are beautiful?" he asked.

"What?" I didn't know how to answer that, but I felt a flush creep over my cheeks.

Greyson nodded toward a corner of the room near a refreshment table. "Is that him?"

There were four girls, teenagers, standing around. Then I saw my brother. They were all laughing and my brother obviously had their attention.

I squeezed my eyes tightly closed. "Unfortunately, yes."

"That's a good thing, right?" He said, not waiting for an answer. "He's having a good time. So should we."

Three couples had made their way out to the middle of the floor and were slow dancing.

"We could dance," he said.

"I do not know how to dance like that."

He just stared at me.

"I can waltz," I said quickly.

Greyson laughed and took me by the hand.

"Don't worry," he said. "You've got this." Then he led me to the edge of the dance floor and pulled me close. One hand on my waist, the other clasping my hand. Not knowing what else to do, I put my left hand on his shoulder. We weren't touching otherwise, but we were close.

He smelled so good. Like leather and soap and… jet fuel. I smiled. When had I started liking the scent of jet fuel?

"You're a natural," he said.

I relaxed. This was actually quite nice. I could, however, see why our tutor had not taught us to dance like this. It was simply swaying in what could be a rather intimate way.

"Is this a good time for you tell me your secret?"

Was it? I didn't know what his reaction would be. I decided to take it slowly. And on second thought, I would not start at the beginning.

"First of all, I don't know how my brother found me. We're from the east side of Canada."

"Young people are quite resourceful," he said with barely a hitch. "with technology."

"I guess they are. I sent him emails from a library in Boulder." I looked around as I spoke, making sure no one was listening in. Just in case.

"That seems safe enough."

"You would think so," I said. "And yet he found me anyway."

"You're happy to see him though."

The song changed, but we didn't. We just kept dancing… swaying actually.

"I'm very happy to see him. But he hasn't told me what he's doing here."

"Looking for you, I would imagine."

I took a deep breath.

"Let's get some punch," he said. "Or whatever it is they're serving here."

"Good idea," I said.

Greyson was not only breathtakingly handsome, he was kind and thoughtful.

We walked hand in hand to the refreshment table.

Abby stood behind it. She broke into a huge grin when she saw Greyson. "You made it," she said.

Greyson nodded once. "Two cups of champagne punch please."

Abby kept the smile on her face but I saw the disappointing glance she sent in my direction. I didn't blame her. Greyson was most definitely the most handsome man here tonight.

We took our punch and went to stand at the edge of the room.

"This is so different from Houston," he said.

"How so?"

"If I were in Houston right now, I'd be with my family."

"Oh." I took a sip of the champagne. "I don't think you ever really said why you're here."

He brought a hand to his lips and kissed the backs of my fingers. "I thought it might be evident by now."

I looked away from his mesmerizing gaze and remembered who I was and why I was here.

Greyson Fleming didn't fit into the equation. I had to figure just who I was first.

36

GREYSON

"*I* can keep you safe, you know."

"So you said."

Did I? I released Noelle's hand after a quick squeeze and after straightening my tie, loosening it a bit, took another sip of the champagne. It was more punch than champagne. Just a touch of champagne. Probably some ginger ale, too.

The Christmas music changed into something festive. Thank goodness. The mournful tunes played with my emotions, mostly leaving me feeling everything from nostalgic to sad to hopeful to everything in between.

But right now, I was feeling almost overwhelmingly... happy. It made no sense, really. I should, by all rights, be at home, spending Christmas Eve with my family. My grandfather, grandmother, parents, siblings, cousins. They would all be there tonight. Then tomorrow they would spend the day with their own smaller families.

But instead, I was thousands of miles away spending time with strangers. It wasn't so much the little town that I was drawn to. I could take it or leave it and when it got right down to it, I was a city boy. It was Noelle. She was the constant holding me here.

"You should be with your family," she said, still not looking at me.

"Noelle," I said. It didn't come out as a question or a statement, but somewhere in between and I didn't know what my intent was.

She blinked rapidly, then turned and met my gaze. Her emerald green eyes were so beautiful, but at the moment they were filled with unshed tears.

"Don't be sad," I said, lightly touching a finger to the delicate skin just below one of her eyes.

She took a deep ragged breath. "I had to leave my home," she said.

"Why?"

"My father."

My thoughts scattered in a hundred different directions, all of them bad.

"You're doing that thing again," I said. "Telling me just enough to make my imagination run out of control."

She smiled a little. Enough that I knew she was going to be okay. Taking a deep breath, she began to tell me her story.

"My family's home is on an island. The island has been in the family for hundreds of years."

She paused, looking sideways at me, gauging for a reaction.

"It must be very old then."

"It is very old. But it's in very good condition." She looked at me with a little smile.

I waited. Not saying anything. I didn't know what to say.

"My father hasn't been a very good steward of the property. He and my mother have lived a bit extravagantly."

I nodded. We waited while a couple holding hands passed by.

"Your family is in financial trouble?" I asked, knowing it

was a very personal question, but it seemed like this was where she was headed.

But she didn't seem offended. "Yes," she said. "Exactly."

"Is that why you left? To earn money for the family?"

She looked at me with a curious expression as though that thought hadn't really occurred to her. "No. It was not like that."

"How was it then?"

"I don't know." She looked up, blinking rapidly. "I just needed to leave."

I nodded, but I didn't understand. Not even a little.

"So... what now?"

Taking a deep breath, she looked back into my eyes. "I don't really know. I only know that there is only one way to save my family's heritage."

"What way is that?" I asked.

"I have to marry the man I'm betrothed to."

37

NOELLE

The crowd was thinning as people began to leave the gym decorated in twinkling, colorful lights. I heard someone say something about the weather starting to get bad. It was going to snow and no one wanted to get stuck at the high school gym on Christmas Eve when they could be home getting ready for Santa.

But Greyson and I didn't move. We sat there, hand in hand even as someone turned off the music, more than a hint that it was time to go.

"Betrothed?" Greyson asked, turning on the bench to face me. "What does that even mean?"

It would have been funny. Except that it wasn't.

"It means that my father signed an agreement with a man... a neighbor for me to marry his son."

Greyson shook his head. "It's the twenty-first century. He can't make you marry anyone."

"You are right, of course. But there is no other way for us to get the money to save our island. Our home."

"Your family could live somewhere else. Maybe."

"I do not think you understand. Our home has been in the family for hundreds of years."

"I get that. I do. Tradition is very important. But it's not worth you marrying someone you don't... love."

I didn't say anything. He didn't understand.

"But do you?" he asked. "Do you love him?"

"Do I love who?"

"Your betrothed. Or fiancé. Or whatever."

I looked at him like he had grown two heads. He just shrugged. "It's kind of important."

"I would think it would be," I said. "And THAT is why I left the island. That is why I left everything behind."

"Noelle," he said. "I want to understand. I do. But..."

I took both his hands in mine and looked into his deep, sparkling blue eyes.

"I have never met him."

It took him a second to comprehend my words. He pulled back a little. My worst fear. That he would think my family crazy and run from here.

"Surely you can't be serious."

"But I am. My father arranged all this. He put saving our home on my shoulders."

"He can't do that."

"But he did." I stood up. "So I left. I ran away."

He stood up with me and we walked to the coat check to get our coats. I was having trouble getting the words out.

I missed home. I hadn't realized just how much until this minute.

We took our coats and he held mine while I slipped my arms in the warm sleeves.

"Where's my brother?" I asked, looking around, a bit belatedly.

"I think he left with one of the girls."

"He's only sixteen," I said with a groan.

"I remember being sixteen," Greyson said wistfully.

"Stop it." I slapped playfully at him.

"What?" he said. "I feel a little bit like I'm sixteen now."

"You do not."

Greyson laughed as we stepped outside into the freezing cold, the wind slicing into us.

The beauty of the snow falling along with the sparkling, twinkling lights nearly took my breath away.

"It's beautiful," I said.

"It's the magic of Christmas Eve," he said.

I nodded. "The most magical time of the year."

We hurried toward the ice cream shop and my apartment.

I was a little worried about Nicholas, but he'd made it this far without me even knowing he had left home, so I knew that any worry was misplaced.

My hands shook with cold as I opened the door and stepped inside. I glancing longingly at the cold fireplace, but I had just never gotten around to it.

We went upstairs to my little apartment, hung up our coats, and turned on the tea kettle.

While the water heated, we didn't talk. I enjoyed the companionable silence. Of not feeling pressured to say anything when I didn't know what to say.

I had told Greyson so much, but there were some things I hadn't told him.

As we sat on the sofa with our warm mugs, Greyson just looked at me.

"I do have one question," Greyson said, squeezing my hand. "Why is there a cloak in your hall closet?"

38

GREYSON

*A*s we sat in Noelle's living room on the tattered sofa with the beautiful view of the falling snow out the windows, I held my warm mug tightly in my hands and reflected on what she had told me.

I understood about the importance of family. My family had always been everything to me.

I could not, however, imagine being coerced into marrying someone to save my family's legacy. I would do a lot of things for them. But would I do that?

I hoped that was something I never had to find out. I would not want to be in Noelle's shoes.

I wondered if she was sending money home. I wondered a lot of things.

Living on an island in an old house sounded like the worst kind of childhood. I'd been fortunate. So very fortunate. I had grown up with money never being an issue for anything. It was just something I didn't have to think about.

Fortunate. I was fortunate.

If there was anything I could do to help Noelle and her family I would. But marrying someone she'd never met was something I couldn't fathom. It was something I couldn't help her with if that was what she was going to do.

"I couldn't do it," she said. "I couldn't marry him. My father insisted. But I couldn't do it."

"I've very proud of you for standing your ground and getting away."

"I still feel like there must be something I can do to help my family. But not that."

"No," I said. "Not that. Don't do that."

She smiled a little, just a little.

"I could never do that," she said. "Especially not now."

"Since you met me, right?

She looked at me curiously, but didn't answer.

"Things are different here. We—my brother and I—were sheltered on the island. Sheltered from everything, both good and bad."

"I'm sorry," I said.

"I never thought I'd own an ice cream shop," she said with a little smile.

"I would think not. You said it was something of an accident."

"One of those things a person just falls into."

Sort of like meeting her.

"Do you think you'll go back?" I asked. "To the island."

"I have to go back," she said. "I have duties."

"Please tell me you aren't saying you have a duty to marry that neighbor's son."

"No," she said. "Not that."

"What kind of duties?"

She took a deep breath.

"Eventually I have to go back. Eventually my brother and I have to return to the island and take care of things."

I didn't know how I would feel about going home if my

father was forcing me to marry someone I'd never even met. But I suppose it could happen.

There were worse things.

"There's something else I should probably tell you."

"There's more?"

She smiled. "Unfortunately, yes."

"Alright," I said, straightening up and pretending to prepare myself. For what I didn't know. I hoped it wasn't some other mayhem.

"Before everything—the world—became modern… or so they told me." She hesitated. "Maybe I shouldn't tell you this."

"Now you can't not tell me," I said.

"You're right. You deserve to know the whole story."

"It can't be that bad. Can it?"

"It's probably not even all that important."

"Okay," I said, forcing myself to look unconcerned.

Then she just told me.

"My father is technically the king of the island. So I'm technically a princess."

"Noelle," I said. "Maybe you should tell me a little more about what kind of island it is that you grew up on."

"Maybe," she said with a little nod.

39

NOELLE

*C*hristmas Day dawned with a fresh coating of snow. Getting up, I went to the window, put my hands against the cold window ledge, and gazed out toward the tall rugged mountain peaks that surrounded the little valley that was Whiskey Springs. A layer of clouds hovered across that valley like a misty lake.

Every day the view was different. That was one thing I liked about living here. The view of the ocean out the window where I had grown up looked relatively the same about ninety percent of the time. I even liked storms simply because they changed the landscape.

I turned from the window. Even though the shop downstairs was closed, I had a lot to do today. Even on Christmas Day.

And I had two guests in my living room.

My brother had wandered home looking happy as a lark, apparently taking full advantage of his freedom. I still didn't know how he had found me.

But I was going to catch him early this morning before he had time to run off again to do whatever it was he was doing with his new friends. I needed to know. He needed to talk to me.

After showering and getting dressed, I opened my bedroom door and stepped out.

Greyson stood at the stove making... an omelet? I stepped closer. Surely I was seeing this wrong.

My little brother—not so little anymore—sat at my white wooden antique kitchen table, the top stained by people now forgotten, drinking a cup of coffee and the two of them were laughing at something.

Making breakfast and laughing.

"What—?" I didn't even know I had any ingredients to make an omelet. "How—?"

They looked at me, then each other, then back at me.

Both of them looked so terribly guilty that I had to put a hand over my mouth to keep from laughing out loud.

"You're in time for breakfast," Greyson said.

"I see that."

"Have a seat."

I didn't even ask. This was one of those Christmas Day surprises that wasn't to be questioned.

As I sat down in a chair next to my brother, Greyson poured coffee into my favorite mug waiting on the counter. He added a dash of milk and sweetener, without even asking. It was no coffee shop latte, but the fact that Greyson made it for me, made it even better than any latte.

"Merry Christmas," he said with a grin.

"Merry Christmas." My heart warmed.

I didn't know how it had happened, but somehow Greyson Fleming was here in my little apartment along with my brother. The two people in the world that I cared the most about.

It was little bit odd because I had known one of them my whole life and the other only a few days.

As Greyson scooped up the omelets, I turned to Nicholas.

"You have to tell me," I said. "How did you find me?"

Nicholas made a face. He pulled out his cell phone and put it on the table.

"You have your cell phone?" he asked.

"Of course." I took my phone from my jacket pocket and laid it next to his.

He held up his phone. Clicked on an app called "Find My."

And there I was on his phone. Right there. A little photo putting me right here in Whiskey Springs.

He leaned toward me and whispered in a stage whisper. "I've known all along," he said.

I didn't gasp, at least I didn't think I did. Not out loud.

"All this time?" I whispered, only because I couldn't quite get my voice to work.

Nicholas nodded.

I cleared my voice. "And Father?"

"Of course." He shrugged as though it was nothing. "He had you followed until you appeared to be safe."

I had been right. I had seen someone watching me on occasion. I didn't know whether to feel relieved or angry. I decided to go with aghast.

And how exactly did Father decide that I was safe? But I bit my lip. I had more important information to find out.

Greyson set the plates in front of us and sat down in the chair next to me. He grinned at me as he sat down. Warm shivers ran down my smile and I smiled back.

"This is absolutely delicious," I said, looking over at Greyson after tasting the omelet—where he got eggs, peppers, and bacon I would never know.

"I'm so glad you like it."

Then I turned back to my brother and the issue at hand.

"Did Father send you to bring me home?" I asked, keeping my tone even.

"No," Nicholas said between bites. "Father has taken on a whole new plan."

"What kind of plan?" I held my fork halfway to my mouth. So much for an even tone.

"I don't know," Nicholas said with all the nonchalance of a sixteen-year-old boy. "Something that doesn't involve you getting married. That much I know."

"How did you get away?"

"Father said it was time for me to go find my own way."

I took a bite of omelet. Considered.

"Father did not say that."

Nicholas shrugged. "He thinks I came to visit you for Christmas."

"Oh." And that was exactly what he was doing. It seemed like there might be more to the story, but he would tell me in his own good time.

"So she's no longer betrothed?" Greyson asked.

"Nah," Nicholas said. "That didn't work out."

I looked at Greyson and just laughed.

For almost a whole year I had been worried about something that I didn't need to worry about at all.

40

GREYSON

I ran a hand along one of the snags on the well-worn, but comfortable sofa where I sat with Noelle, both us of holding flutes of bubbly champagne.

We sat in front of the fireplace in her apartment. The General Store in town was open and I had snagged some firewood and kindling earlier in the day. It seemed like a waste of a good fireplace to not use it.

I liked her apartment a whole lot better with the coziness of a fire burning.

And I especially liked it that we were alone. Nicholas had somehow already found himself a girlfriend in town and was at her home for the evening.

"A cat used to live here," I said.

"Yes," Noelle said. "Smedley."

"Wait." I leaned forward to face her. "Smedley. As in Smedley's Ice Cream shop?"

"Yes." She smiled wistfully. "The owner—the previous owner—took Smedley with her to Florida."

"You miss him."

She nodded. "He lived here, you know. He would even sleep with me at night."

Lucky cat.

The fire crackled and the orange flames licked at the logs. I would have to add more wood in a few minutes.

But right now, I just wanted to sit here next to Noelle. Reaching over, I took her hand in mine.

"How are you?" I asked. "With everything?"

"I'm relieved." She blew out a breath. "I don't even care if my father had me tracked. I don't have to worry about him finding me and dragging me back to LaFleur Island to marry a man I've never met."

"LaFleur Island? Your island has a name."

She smiled at me. "Our home has a name."

"It does not." I thought about my grandparents' house. Did it have a name? I was pretty sure it didn't. "What's it called?"

She laughed. "LaFleur Castle."

"Come here," I said, pulling her toward me.

"What?"

I took her flute and set it on the coffee table.

I looked into her eyes. "There's something I'd like to do that I have never done before."

"What's that?"

I ran my thumb lightly over her cheek, then tucked a strand of hair behind her ear.

"I have never kissed a princess."

"Well," she said with a charming, dangerously charming, smile. "Every man should kiss a princess at one time or another."

I ran my finger lightly over her lips.

"No," I said. "I don't think so. Not every man. Just a privileged few."

"Is that so?" she asked.

"That is so. And..." I said. "Did you know that once a man kisses a princess, it's forever?"

"I did not know that," she said. "Is that sort of like when a princess kisses a frog and he turns into a prince?"

I tilted my head a little. Then shook my head with a little shrug.

I didn't need to understand the logic.

I just smiled.

And then I kissed her.

EPILOGUE
NOELLE

One Year Later
Christmas Eve

I stood at the window and looked down at the street below. This window wasn't here last year, but Greyson and I, with the help of his older sister's husband, Charlie—an engineer, knocked out a wall and added a floor to ceiling window that looked out over Main Street.

Greyson was running late, but his ETA was in exactly... I glanced at the new "Find My" app on my phone... seven minutes.

He'd had a flight to Houston today, then tomorrow, the two of us were flying back to Houston to spend Christmas with his family.

He hadn't said who his client was today. He usually told me something about his passengers. We pretty much told each other everything.

He told me about his passengers and I told him about my customers. When he wasn't flying, he worked with me in the ice cream shop.

So, now Whiskey Springs now had two pilots. Daniel Fleming and Greyson Fleming. The Whiskey Springs Airport was taking on quite a life of itself. The word was that Skye Travels was going to be bringing in another airplane and leaving it here along with the other one.

Their other brother Dr. Jack Fleming also lived here.

I watched the twinkling, sparkly lights that covered everything that didn't move. Whiskey Springs was synonymous with Christmas. Everything else was draped with a wreath or garland or some other holiday decoration.

I caught a glimpse of Greyson's white BMW as it turned into the driveway to the parking spot behind the building.

He was a couple of minutes early. I turned away from the window and hurried down the stairs to the back door. As I unlocked the door, I caught a glimpse of the sparkly round diamond on my left hand and smiled to myself. I peeked out the window as I waited impatiently for Greyson. I'd go outside, but I had learned the hard way that it was much warmer to wait inside.

A couple of minutes later, I heard his footsteps as he strode to the door. I turned the knob and stepped aside, then closed the door behind him, closing out the icy cold air, misting with early hints of snow, as well.

Greyson came in, set a lidded wicker basket on the floor, and grabbed me up in his arms. He twirled me around, my feet leaving the floor.

"I missed you," he said, setting me back on the floor, kissing my cheeks, my eyelids, then my lips.

"You just saw me this morning," I said, but I was delighted that he was happy to see me.

"Let's go upstairs," he said. "I have a present for you."

I looked down at the basket. "What is it?"

"Uh uh. You have to come upstairs before you open the

basket." He grabbed it up by the handle with one hand and took one of my hands with the other.

After we made it upstairs and closed our apartment door behind us, he hugged me again and kissed me just as his lips touched mine.

I froze. And listened.

"Did you hear a cat?" I asked.

"Did you?" he asked against the corner of my lips.

"Meeeooow."

"I definitely heard a cat," I said. "Most definitely."

Taking my hand, he led me to the sofa to sit beside him.

Then he leaned forward and lifted the lid from the basket. A little black and white kitten jumped out. Its little face was white on one side and black on the other.

"What?" I asked, looking from the kitten to him and back again. Delighted.

Greyson picked up the kitten and handed her to me.

I snuggled it close to me and looked up at Greyson with my heart in my throat.

"I thought since Smedley's Ice Cream Shop is named after a cat, there should be a cat," he said.

I held the kitten up and looked into its clear blue eyes.

"There's only one problem," he said.

"What's that?" I asked, keeping my gaze on the kitten.

"This one is a girl."

The kitten purred and snuggled her head against me, stealing my heart. I'd name her Medley. She would be the new Smedley's Ice Cream shop ambassador... and our new roommate.

"It's okay," I said, smiling up at Greyson. "She has your eyes."

Keep Reading for a preview of
SECOND CHANCE KISSES...

PREVIEW SECOND CHANCE KISSES

Madison Worthington

This was not happening.

Not in a hundred years.

I stared at the schedule on the computer screen in front me. The caller on the other end of the phone line forgotten.

The least of my problems.

I forgot to breathe. Or maybe I just couldn't get any air.

How many Kade Johnsons were there?

How many Kade Samuel Johnsons?

How many Kade Samuel Johnsons who were pilots?

"Hello?"

Right. I was scheduling a flight for Markus Peters. One of Skye Travel's best customers.

Shit.

"I'm so sorry Mr. Peters. There was a glitch in the phone line." There was actually a glitch in my brain.

It had been eight years since I'd seen Kade Johnson.

Eight years.

And not a day in those eight years had passed that I hadn't

had at least a fleeting thought of Kade Johnson in one way or another.

I put Mr. Peters on speaker and keyed in his information. He now had a flight to Florida with his family scheduled for Friday.

With Kade Johnson in the pilot's seat.

My little brother, Quinn, was going to hear about this. Had Quinn lost his mind?

"Thank you, Mr. Peters, for flying Skye Travels. We'll see you Friday."

I clicked off the phone and looked toward the conference room.

Fortunately for Quinn, he was tied up in a meeting for the next... I glanced at my watch... hour or so.

And by then, I'd be heading out.

It was only my first day on the job—sort of, but I'd been doing this work on and off, since I was a senior in high school.

A questionable perk of being the boss's daughter.

My father, Noah Worthington, believed his children should work like everyone else.

He didn't want us growing up soft, living off his money. And all five of his children had careers.

The only questionable one, though, was my little brother Quinn.

He'd gotten his business degree, then somehow slid right into the company as vice-president.

He claimed to be following in our father's footsteps, but I seemed to be the only one who noticed that Quinn had never flown an airplane.

Our father, however, was a well-known and respected pilot and had formed his company, Skye Travels, based on that reputation.

I could see the tarmac from here. Close enough that the

office carried the comforting scent of jet fuel. But right now even that wasn't enough to calm my nerves.

I had to get through the next hour. Then I could figure out what to do about this Kade Johnson thing.

I straightened up what was going to be my workspace for the next three months and checked my phone messages.

I had one text from my best friend Emily.

EMILY: *Are you off yet?*

ME: *Not yet. One hour left.*

EMILY: *Drinks at the Skyhouse?*

She completely read my mind. I'd only been back in town a few days and hadn't seen my best friend yet.

ME: *OMG. Yes.*

EMILY: *See you there.*

My fingers hovered over the keys. But I set my phone down. I wasn't ready to tell her about Kade. I was still processing it myself and I didn't need Emily's opinion tossed into my brain just yet.

Quinn stuck his head out of the conference room across the hall.

"Madison? Would you make some copies for us?"

"Of course." I put a big fake smile on my face for the benefit of the two men who were meeting with Quinn as I took the envelope from him.

The men were from a big marketing firm and Quinn was meeting them to set up a contract. I had to give Quinn credit. He was good at schmoozing.

But seriously. Quinn was taking advantage of me.

I should have a nameplate made for the receptionist desk.

Dr. Madison Worthington.

I squared my shoulders. I'd done it to myself. I was the one who'd volunteered to help out until he could hire someone for the summer. And then I'd be the one to train the new person.

The receptionist they'd had for years had retired last week. I had trained her myself during the summer before I left for graduate school. I seriously think she waited until she knew I was coming in for the summer before she announced it.

I didn't blame her. This way I was the one doing the training.

My father's work ethic was firmly cemented in my psyche.

I didn't begrudge it. That work ethic was what had gotten me through undergrad in three years. Then graduate school.

After getting my license to practice psychology, I'd done some teaching at Houston Community College and discovered that I liked it. Okay. Loved it.

At first, I couldn't believe they were paying me to do something that was so much fun.

It hadn't taken me long to land a full-time teaching job.

In Denver.

I had three months before I had to show up for new faculty orientation.

Since I already had my apartment secured, I had some time on my hands.

The copy room was at the other end of the office suite. Past the elevator.

Just as I stepped past the elevator, it dinged.

Skye Travels was known for not only its efficiency, but also its Houston hospitality.

I turned, holding the brown envelope Quinn had handed me against my chest and prepared to greet whoever stepped off the elevator.

But also, Quinn was waiting.

I took a step backwards.

The elevator doors opened.

And I froze.

Kade Samuel Johnson stepped off the elevator.

I was having that breathing problem again.

Maybe I should see a doctor about that.

But I already knew it was full-fledged anxiety.

And I knew how to treat it. I was a psychologist after all.

Take a deep breath.

Kade stepped out of the elevator. Stopped and looked right at me.

It was almost like he'd known I was standing there.

He wouldn't have known, of course.

Couldn't have known.

He looked at me blankly.

He didn't even recognize me.

We'd been together for three years and he didn't even recognize me.

I clamped down every thought that came to my head.

Kade worked here now.

My stupid, inconsiderate, clueless brother had hired him.

So I just turned around.

I turned around and continued to the copy room.

I wasn't about to let Kade Johnson know that I'd thought about him every day when he couldn't even have the decency to recognize me.

Sure. It had been eight years.

Sure. Instead of actually breaking up, we'd drifted apart.

But still.

I stepped into the copy room and opened the envelope.

My hands were shaking too much for me to do the simple task of pulling the papers out of the envelope and my eyes wouldn't focus.

Damn it.

This was not going to get the best of me.

I yelped as the envelope sliced across my right index finger giving me a paper cut.

I dropped the envelope onto the copier and stuck my bleeding finger in my mouth.

When I'd gotten up this morning, I'd had no idea that this would be the day I'd see Kade Johnson again.

And all the psychological training in the world was useless.

Kade Johnson

I recognized Madison immediately, of course.

But I swear my body knew she was there before I did.

As soon as the elevator dinged and the door opened, it knew.

I'd always liked the scent of jet fuel, but it had never been a turn on.

Not like that.

It was definitely Madison.

By the time my brain caught up, she'd turned around and walked away.

My first instinct was to follow her. And I even took two steps forward before my logical brain reminded me that my instinct was eight years out of date.

She'd always been pretty. With a quick smile.

But the Madison who'd just walked away from me was not pretty. She was drop dead gorgeous.

Long, brunette mermaid hair. That perfect heart-shaped face. Lips that naturally turned up at the corners.

And a tight black skirt that did everything to remind me what I knew about that body beneath it.

She was wearing a white button-down shirt tucked into that skirt, revealing her narrow waist.

I bet I could still wrap my hands around that waist.

But I worked here now. And she was the boss's daughter.

I had to keep it together.

And keep it in my pants.

I needed a minute before I walked down to reception to meet up with Quinn.

The last thing I needed was to walk into my new office with a hard-on.

I'd only met Quinn Worthington once and during the interview calls, neither one of us had mentioned my previous relationship with his sister. It was possible he didn't even remember me from back then.

Not likely. But certainly possible.

He was younger than I was. Five years? Maybe more.

And when I'd been with Madison, Quinn had been away at a boarding school or some such to prep him for college.

It occurred to me then that Quinn might have hired me without telling Madison.

And if Madison worked here...

I thought she'd be far away from here by now.

I'd seen enough social media updates—not stalking—to know that she'd finished her degree in psychology.

She'd finished it just like she'd set out to do.

Madison completed everything she set out to do. It was one of the many things I admired about her.

Unfortunately, though, it had been the end of our relationship.

We'd decided not to do the whole long distance thing.

I don't know what she'd been thinking, but I always sort of thought we were on a break.

I'd dated, of course. It had been eight years after all and a man had needs.

But I'd never let myself get serious with anyone.

Was it because of Madison?

Not that I would ever admit it.

I turned left and went toward what looked like a lobby. All my interviews and discussions had been via FaceTime. My reputation was good enough to get me a job anywhere in the industry.

But life happened and I needed to be closer to home.

There was no one at the receptionist's desk. Quinn was in the glass-walled conference room on the other end of the lobby with two men.

I took a seat on one of the little sofas in the spacious lobby. This whole side of the office had floor to ceiling windows overlooking the tarmac.

I had an involuntary little sense of excitement. This third floor office space was perfect.

I should have known Noah Worthington would do it right. The man had gone from being a commercial pilot—like me—to owning a fleet of small jets. He had started out in Dallas/Fort Worth, but for some unknown reason, he'd moved his main office to Houston.

Rumors suggested it had something to do with his wife Savannah. And apparently they were living in Houston now.

The receptionist must have already left for the day. Not a problem. I didn't have anything else I had to do today.

I stretched out my legs and pulled out my iPad. Scrolled idly through my emails.

But. Damn it. I couldn't concentrate.

Madison was somewhere in this office. I know she recognized me, but she'd turned walked away.

At the sound of feminine heels coming toward me from the elevator area, I looked up.

And watched as Madison walked straight toward me.

I stood up. Bad idea.

All the blood had rushed to my center.

Then she smiled and I nearly came undone.

Madison

Kade Johnson had gotten even more handsome with age. But it was like that with guys.

He was wearing black slacks and a white button-down

shirt. Basic pilot attire. Same basic outfit I was wearing except that I was wearing a skirt and heels, of course.

Was that why I had butterflies in my stomach? Just because we were wearing the same kind of clothes?

Of course not. Sometimes I put too much into all the psychological theories that had been hammered into my head.

He recognized me now. I could see it all over his face.

It had certainly taken him long enough.

I afforded him the same hospitality I'd give anyone visiting my father's company.

Only, he was doing more than just visiting. And since I was going to be working here for the next three months, I had no choice but to be cordial.

We'd parted as friends and promised to stay in touch.

That promise had been made eight years ago and I hadn't heard from him since that day we'd said good-bye in the parking lot of our favorite taco pub.

"Hello Kade," I said.

"Hello Madison." He smiled back.

I was impressed by how quickly he'd recovered from not recognizing me.

"You're working here now."

"What are you doing here?"

We both spoke at the same time.

We'd always had an uncanny kind of sync.

Was that how his first day and my first day were the same?

But no, I was being fanciful. I'd worked here on and off as needed over the years and this was the first time Kade had shown up.

It was just a weird quirk of chance.

Unless…

I narrowed my eyes in the direction of the conference room.

Had Quinn orchestrated this?

"Quinn didn't tell you, did he?" Kade asked, echoing my thoughts.

"No," I said. "But I saw your name on the schedule."

"Quinn moves fast," he said.

"We don't like to waste time here at Skye Travels." I held the envelope with the copies close to my chest. Like a shield.

"It's good to see you," he said. "But, seriously, what are you doing here?"

"Working," I said. "If you'll excuse me, I have to get these to Quinn."

I turned and walked straight for the conference door.

Quinn met me there and took the papers off my hands.

I went back to the reception desk, took my seat, and put the headset back on.

I did all this without glancing at Kade one single time.

I could do this.

I could be around him and not focus on him.

I was very pleased with my progress so far.

"Why aren't you somewhere straightening out lives?"

I jumped back, stifling a yelp.

Kade was leaning on the counter, smiling at me.

In my efforts to not look at him, I hadn't seen him move over to the reception desk.

Maybe this was going to be a bit harder than I thought.

Keep Reading SECOND CHANCE KISSES...

Kathryn Kaleigh writes sweet contemporary romance, time travel romance, and historical romance.

kathrynkaleigh.com

CPSIA information can be obtained
at www.ICGtesting.com
Printed in the USA
BVHW060849170223
658730BV00006B/98